# Resilient Hearts

**GLEN KAIPOSU FAITE**

Mortlock Islands, ARO Bougainville

**Paperback ISBN: 978-1-7638456-3-3**

First Published in 2025 by
**First Nations Writers Festival International Limited
T/as First Nations Publishers**

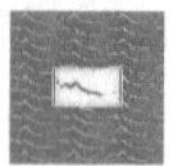

A Registered Charity (ABN 79 655 932 979)

2/53 Junction St, Nowra NSW 2540, Australia
Phone: +61 491 851 353

Email: firstnationswritersfestival@gmail.com
Web: www.firstnationswritersfestival.org
FB: www.facebook.com/firstnationswritersfestival.com

**Cover Design:** Busybird Publishing
**Typeset:** Busybird Publishing
**Cover/back cover photos:** Pixabay, Glen Faite
**Line Edited:** Anna Borsi AM 2025

Printed and bound in Australia by IngramSpark

A catalogue record fpor this book is available from the National Library of Australia

*"Every time news reaches me of disasters affecting
my island, I get frustrated that my people and I can't do
anything to ease all the problems that are affecting my
island and my people due to issues beyond our control."*

*He hopes this story encourages action. "If you are
living in an area that is prone to disasters, speak up and do
something now if you want your people and cultures to be
safe. Even when the Indigenous stories can't be heard, they
can be read. The only time people's ideas make sense is when
the audience settles down and mentally digests
the information through reading."*


*Thank you for reading my book.*


Interview:*https://nit.com.au/18-06-2025/18617/stories-of-culture-and-conflict-win-at-2025-first-nations-writers-festival

# CHARACTER LIST

**Protagonists**

1. **Telakitahuri** – A student from Mortlock Island who, while pursuing his studies in NZ was caught in between his studies, community issues and deciding between Prudence and Tukala. With the latter, his weak heart troubled him for sometimes as he tossed about ideas of who to take as his lifetime partner. His world came crashing when his island was destroyed by the sea. He had to take the challenge to improve life on the island and, he could not have done it all without his true love and others at his back.

2. **Prudence** – a Caucasian student who fell in love with a fellow student who was not of her race. Her love tamed her parents to accept the man she loved. She saw love as something deeper than skin colour and personal attributes. Though the challenges in having to cope with Telakitahuri's commitment to his society, she persevered with her love and travelled thousands of miles just to be with the man she truly loved.

3. **Tukala** – the saying that your true love will not always be yours forever, encompassed the life of Tukala. An arrogant lover who lived on the faith that Telakitahuri would return for her got the shock of her life when things did not turn out as she expected. Luckily traditional arrangements brought her a new lover

that she could not ask more for, despite the torment it silently had on Telakitahuri.

4.  **Telanito** – the best friend of Telakitahuri who went on to marry Tukala in the interest of his parents. Without any insecurity about Telakitahuri and Tukala's past, he rested on his parent's belief that Tukala was the right woman for him. He also built that trust that Tukala will learn to love him over time.

5.  **Sione and Teitione** – Telakitahuri's sister and brother in-law who have been always his pillars of support.

## Antagonist

6.  **Tekata** – a man who for all reasons hated everything that Telakitahuri did. Whilst his reasons were portrayed to be politically motivated, it ran deeper than that. It could be attributed to jealousy or not liking people who try to change the status quo in the village.

Tears freely flowed down his eyes as Telakitahuri stood to receive his vaisonis and hugs from his family, relatives and friends.

There were mournful sobs all around as the villagers gathered on the beach to farewell those who were travelling on MV Tausena, including him. It's been like that every time a ship departed the island of Nukutapu with loved ones. However, the sobbing and wailing now seemed more heart felt than ever before and he could not understand why.

He could not fight back his tears as he was overwhelmed by sadness. One after the other, he fell into their embraces and vaisonis. Then, he felt strong arms embracing him from the back. He turned and the hulking frame of his father, Tearopa, imposed his masculinity just above his manhood. He looked into his eyes and his teary eyes searched the heavens for the right words.

Finally, in a roaring voice that was occasionally choked by sobs, he uttered his farewell as he tightened his embrace. The grip was one he had never felt in the eight years that he's been leaving his family to pursue his education abroad. His farewell and fatherly words of advice gave him goose bumps and more sadness as he tried to comprehend an utterance totally unexpected of him.

"Son, I love you. I don't know if we'll have another opportunity to embrace like this on this beach. Where-ever fate takes us, do not forget your roots and always walk the path that I've shown you. I have a feeling things are not right."

Letting go of his father's embrace was the hardest thing. Like a royal crown, the hau - a leafy branch of a shrub imbued with ancestral energy, adorning his head for their protection during the voyage - shook as he sobbed in great sorrow.

Everyone around him moved in to console him, thinking he was just sad to leave but in fact, it was his father's words that created that uncertainty of sadness.

He pulled up his laplap to get it away from the water's surface and climbed onto the canoe. As those on the beach moved away from the canoe, the paddler cut the sea with incredible strength, moving the vaka away from the shoreline.

He turned back to the shore, and the sight of his father standing on the beach looking at him with eyes flooded with tears broke his heart. He pulled out the laplap that draped over his garment, squeezed it and threw it to those nearest to pass to his father. As the canoe began to take its momentum, he shouted. "Keep that, Papa. As a symbol of our love and the love that I will return for."

In the sadness of the moment, his heart jumped with joy as his father, with teary eyes, lifted the laplap in his hands to signal he has received it well, including his words.

The engine of MV Tausena came alive, shooting black fumes into the air. Young boys, including Telakitahuri, were all on the upper deck, waving laplaps at those at the shore. At that distance, they could see among the coconut palms that lined the shore, laplaps were waved back at them. Those were the last goodbyes of loved ones whom they'll return to see, perhaps after some months or years, as they make it each day in their little paradise.

As the engine revved to momentum, Telakitahuri settled on the wooden bench. Sadly, he watched as the islands began to drift away at the rate of MV Tausena's speed. All of a sudden, he noticed something. He stood up and looked carefully. He realised that the islands were smaller than he once knew. And, the gaps between them were greater than they were in the past.

"I feel for our islands," in the top of his voice, he said to his best friend Telanito, trying to be heard above the roar of the engine.

Not too eager for a conversation, Telanito nodded, with his sight affixed to the distancing islands. Up to that moment, he wasn't sure whether his decision to go to town was right. After leaving school, he had spent most of his time on the island till he decided it was time to find employment in town. With no documents except his grade ten certificate, he hoped an opportunity would present itself.

"You realised the islands are getting smaller?" asked Tekosi, a youth leader whose frequent trips to town were all his initiatives to find opportunities in all aspects for the youths on the island. "We've been experiencing very high seas in past few years and the Disaster Officers who came to assess our situation said climate change was the cause. However, I fail to understand how the change of climate could possibly affect the sea. Believing what you don't know much about can be hard."

The young men were soon joined by others as they discussed the many problems that affected their islands as they begin their voyage to Kieta. "Look, you see that island?" Tekuro asked, another youth who was travelling to seek medical attention, as he pointed to Nukuahare. "It's been cut in the middle and the gap is growing bigger every time strong tides hit the island. I wonder if there's anything our community government could do to stop that erosion getting out of hand. We might lose that island completely."

Then, those who were present on the island, reminisced about that horrible day when the North-East seas brought towering waves that rolled into the island. The expression on their faces said it all as they relived those moments through their stories.

"I've never seen waves of that size come close to the shoreline. On the northern side of the island, the waves normally break onto the reef and roll about fifty metres before they lose their strength and fade out. However, on that day, the waves dug deep and splashed some metres in from where they normally splashed, rolling at a great speed towards the shoreline. The first one rolled five metres into the island and, as it receded, was met by another rolling wave which caused an upheaval in the level of water pushing further into the island. After about five waves, half of the island was inundated with water. Walls of houses were ripped off and properties floated all over the place. We ran around trying our best to save whatever we could. However, the destruction had already been made to the village. That was the worst experience I've had on the island," recalled Telanito.

Telakitahuri was emotional. Those stories only hurt his heart more as he was still to get over the sorrow of leaving loved ones behind. Slowly and calmly, he rose to his feet and moved out of the group of boys. He didn't want any more of those stories. He looked towards the stern. The distance was now great as MV Tausena had been running at 12 knots per hour. He looked to the bow and avananui passage was nearing. To his right Nukerekia, though visibly reduced in size through the viciousness of the sea's cruelty, didn't fail to impress him.

The variety of bird species encircled it like bees desperate for a flower's nectar. He longed to be on that island. It was a perfect picnic spot where the fish would grace the tip of your spear as if daring you. The birds too, would provoke your desire for a dish of eggs by tossing them carelessly on the sand. He promised himself a good picnic on the island on his return home.

As the ship exited Avananui passage and began cutting the sea to its destination, the boys dispersed. It was time to check out their beds for the night and for some, the reality of missing loved ones whom they'd left behind kicked in. Sitting alone, gazing at the endless ocean that seemed to be begging for dear light from the run-away sun, Telakitahuri's mind raced back to the great times he had on the island.

If he didn't value his education, he could have remained on his paradise. He was mesmerised in those moments and the sudden flicking on of the lights forced him out of the other side of reality.

"Holy cow! Its night now," he said to himself, pulling himself up by the guardrails.

The metre high sea produced choppy waves that made him stagger somewhat to his cabin. He opened the door and moderate coolness and air freshener fragrance shot into his face and nostrils. He sat on the lower bed, lay down to test its comfort and then sat up again. He felt that it was too early for a lie down, so he took out his IPad from his accessory bag, connected his Bluetooth headphones, put them over his head and headed to the upper deck.

Several passengers who wanted to enjoy the cool sea breeze sat on the benches. A group of high school boys were enjoying their music, blasted from a small handheld gadget. He didn't want to inhale smoke from their cigarettes so he took the front bench on the port side. He dropped onto the bench, spread out his arms on the backrest and closed his eyes.

Tehine moana's tempo pulsated in rhythm with his heart - a wonderful song that he loved. The trembling and rocking of the boat made him feel that he was dancing to the beat of the music. After some time, he opened his eyes and the million stars in his sight appeared and disappeared behind the canopy of the deck as the ship danced to the tune of the waves.

He could see Kaipea twinkling brightly to the west just above the horizon. This evoked wonderment as to how his ancestors traversed the oceans from their origins of Sopokanatela, through the many islands in the Pacific Ocean to what is now popularly known as the Mortlock Islands.

He opened the Global Positioning System Application in his IPad and took a look at where their journey began. He was mesmerised by the seafaring talent and skills his ancestors possessed and was so proud of them. Without a compass or GPS they navigated the vast oceans establishing territories to support their expanding populations.

His thoughts were interrupted when an announcement came through the P.A system. "Good night, ladies and gentlemen. The mess is now open for dinner. Dinner time is strictly one hour from now." The passengers on that deck were all preparing to head to the mess when Laumana, the Chef on board, told them to remain where they were as his kitchen staff will bring their meals to them.

Also, from Nukutapu, Laumana began his career as a cook in hotels around town but the love of traveling from place to place brought him to MV Tausena. In less than five minutes, the trays of pre-packed dinners and drinks were delivered. Telakitahuri opened his pack.

"Wow, I like this," he exclaimed to himself, turning the half chicken to see how well the other side was burnt in its roasting process. Although the meal was appetising and very fulfilling, he couldn't finish everything. He carefully covered the leftover chicken and left it on the bench.

Returning his headphones to his ears, the playlist resumed. The expressive creativity of a great hakatautai who bragged about the value of his haul at sea, "It's a sablefish, it's a grouper, it's an oilfish - these are the spoils of my fishing techniques."

He thought about the long association his people had with the sea, and how they value their rich culture that was intertwined with it. "How ironic!" he gasped, trying to process everything. The very essence of the life of my people was rebelling against their existence.

Finally, it was time for rest. He staggered to the cabin, opened the door and entered. His cabin mate's nose was humming tunes not far from the engine's roar. He got into his bed, pulled over the sheet and closed his eyes.

The rocking of the boat lullabied him to dreamland.

It was around three o'clock when Telakitahuri was awakened by knocking on the door. Still half asleep, he staggered to the door, opened it and there stood Telanito, neatly dressed and looking like he was off for an occasion.

"Taina, what's up?" he asked as he wiped his eyes. "Taina, we are almost there. The lights of Kieta town can be seen. We could be berthing in one and a half hours-time," responded an overly excited Telanito, so excited about seeing town again after so many years.

"Wait for me on the second deck. I will join you soon," said Telakitahuri as he closed the door behind him and slipped into his jeans. He looked at his cabin mate. He thought of waking him up but then hesitated. He didn't know him at all but he shared a room with him. He wondered what the nature of his visit to the island was.

As he closed the door behind him and supported himself by holding onto the walls and rails on his way up, he thought to himself that he should ask him when he woke up.

Telanito was exactly where he told him to wait for him. A few other passengers who had the eye to stay awake till that time sat on other benches. He slumped beside Telanito and gazed out at the distant lights. They were the sign of modernisation, far from the situation back at home, where unreliable solar systems work beyond their limit to provide for the destitute islanders.

Though rich in marine resources, the intricacies of the rule of government policies and the lack of support to monetise that wealth, left them in a state of helplessness - an example was the regulation of the beche-de-mer.

As the ship moved closer, the brighter the lights became. Laumana saw them and offered the boys a cigarette. Telanito took one. He wasn't a smoker but the excitement of getting to town made him pick up one and light it. Lifting his left leg onto the bench, right hand clinging onto the canopy's support, Laumana puffed and chew his betel nut as he spewed out a verbal narration that seemed like it would never end.

"I was about nine years old when the fight in Bougainville started," he began. "Although we were not affected by the fighting, we suffered from the lack of basic goods and services when the Blockade was enforced. During the Blockade, ships stopped sailing to all the islands in the Atolls District and basic goods like rice, sugar and salt all ran out.

"Once in a while, PNG Navy vessels called in. However, they brought no supplies as they were only monitoring the waters around Bougainville.

"We relied on taro, fish and coconut to keep us going. The teachers taught without receiving their salaries and we would go to school every day without knowing the hardship our poor teachers faced each day. They gave us the sweetest smiles, the best lessons and all the love they could offer without the slightest expression of their desperate situation. It was like they had a purpose for their sacrifice.

"Everything seemed normal for us, little children, except that there was no rice and tea. I am so glad that now we are independent even though it took so long," recounted Laumana of his experience of the pre-independence period.

The many stories that he told captivated the boys' interest, only to be interrupted by the P.A system that came alive with instructions to throw the lines ashore, and MV Tausena carefully maneuvered to berth at the Kieta wharf. It had been a cold night for those who lay on the ship. Cool breezes from the Kieta Mountains brought chills to the islanders who were not used to such.

As dawn approached some shivered their way home, desperate for a warm bath or a cup of coffee. While others like Telakitahuri and Telanito, wriggled on their beds, waiting for the resumption of taxis and buses.

Then, it was time to move. Picking up their stuff, they exited their rooms to find each other on the deck. The queue of islanders ready for their turn to climb down the gangway, slowed their haste to get to their waiting taxi. As they stood beside the taxi, Telakitahuri weighed up whether he should check into Bovotel in Arawa or head to his sister's place to await his flight. He felt that the latter was the best option as he would leave his best friend a place to stay when he departed for New Zealand.

For the last three years, he had been studying for a Bachelor's Degree in Development Studies at Massey University under a scholarship program initiated by the Member for Atolls and the New Zealand Ambassador to Bougainville. The scholarship was established for the minority Polynesian students of Bougainville who spoke the Te Nahoa language - a Polynesian Outlier Language spoken by the people of Taku, Nukumanu and Nuguria, mutually intelligible to many Polynesian speakers.

The program aimed to upskill recipients so that they could return and support their people to address issues that kept marginalising or moving them to the periphery of society, being a minority group in a predominantly Melanesian nation. The program took care of his travelling expenses, accommodation and allowances.

After a 20-minute ride, the taxi pulled up outside his sister's place at Toniva. For over five years Teitione and Sione had been living there, where Sione worked in the government. Telakitahuri and Telanito climbed out of the taxi and were greeted by the savory scent of food coming from the house. Their discomforted tummies grumbled due to the rocking of the boat and yearned for delicious food. The dried salted fish and baked sosoro, made from giant taro, didn't seemed appetising to them as they took them out of the taxi. But they knew the family loved them and, in a few days, they would be craving for them.

"Wow, nice house," cried Telanito as he stood admiring the house while Telakitahuri moved forward to meet and greet his family. Their well-constructed brick house was a stone's throw away from the seashore with a lawn big enough for another house. As Sione ushered them into the house where the table was all set for their breakfast, Telanito's eyes wondered around, fascinated by everything that he saw. He was still to get over the surreal feeling that he had made it to town after many years in the village.

Taking their seats, they indulged in their breakfast as they chatted. It was the best meal Telanito had had for a long time. As they ate, Telakitahuri relived great moments he had in the village to the amusement of the family. They were so eager to hear more about the village but had to cut the stories short as Sione had to go to work and little nephews Mete and Tamauhi had to go to school.

"Uncle, can you sleep with me in my room?" asked six-year-old Mete. "I want to spend time with you before you return overseas."

"I'm all right with that, as long as there is enough space for your other uncle here to sleep," he cheerfully responded to the little boy, and patted them both on the head. "I'm so proud of you two."

"Telanito can sleep with Tamauhi in his room," interjected the boys' mother.

As soon as his in-law's car was out, Telakitahuri turned the topic to their father. He was emotional as he spoke. Their biggest worry was that since the passing of their mother two years ago, their father had been living alone in the village with their relatives. He had refused requests from his daughter and son-in-law to come and live with them in town. Their father had always been an island man who rarely ventured out of Nukutoa, unless he had a very good reason.

"While I'm gone overseas, I'd like you to continue checking on him every now and then. I have given him a tablet so you can have video calls with him. He seemed fine. But I was somewhat confused by what he said to me on my departure," he uttered with great pain. "The loss of our mother greatly affected him however; he always maintained that he was coping with life without mother."

The discussions about their father put them through some emotions. Life on the island has toughened and it was no longer like before, especially with climate change impacting the lives of the islanders. The taros were no longer growing healthily as they used to be due to the salt in the soil, the frequent strong winds prevented men from venturing far into the sea and many other climate change issues had changed the lifestyle of the islanders.

"As life gets tough on the island, I don't want father to experience any problems," said Telakitahuri. "I'll share my allowances with him from time to time. Many small shops in the village now have EFTPOS therefore I will need you to wire his money to him when I send it over."

"Are you sure you will be able to sustain your living there if you share your allowances with father?" queried Teitione with great concern. She pitied Telakitahuri for the suffering he might encounter in a foreign land, especially compared to their father, who had extended family around him to help in case he encountered any serious problem.

"The Bougainville currency is still making its way up against the New Zealand dollar so don't worry, I'll cope," he said, nodding his head as assurance that he would be all right. With the increase in GDP in Bougainville, the local currency had been making good progress against foreign currencies and things were looking positive with the opening of some mines, increase in quality cocoa production including the opening of a chocolate factory and many other impact projects such as the opening of the Atolls seaweed cool rooms and other projects soon to realise their full potential.

The theories that Bougainville would not fare well in the world economic space like many other small nations, had been proven all wrong. The resources of the newest nation and the people's ingenuity have been the source of the progress Bougainville has been experiencing since it got its independence.

It was around midday when Telanito remembered that he had a box of dried, salted fish to deliver to his uncle at Arawa. He carried the box and they headed to the bus stop. A group of boys from the Atolls were there at the bus stop. They too were heading to Arawa for their training sessions in various sporting codes. An aura of sportsmanship surrounded them as they held onto their sporting gear and in the best shape of sportsmen.

A bus pulled up. One by one they got in and their journey to Arawa began.

"Hi Taina, just letting you know that if I make the Bougainville Karate team to the Pacific Karate Championships in New Zealand, I might get to meet you there. I've been selected to represent the Atolls in the regional tournament in Buka, and if I fight well, I will be in the team," boasted Kahi, sitting sideways so he could look Telakitahuri in the eyes as he went on about his ambitions.

Telakitahuri was so used to his frivolous blabbering and pretended to be very interested. He knew him well while they were growing up on the island.

Finally, the bus pulled up at the main Arawa town bus station. Again, one by one they climbed down and waited for Telakitahuri who had volunteered to pay for their fares. After sorting that out, they walked a short distance where he asked them to listen to what he had in mind.

"My tainas, I see that some of you are in town for no good reason at all. If city life is what you prefer, make an effort to find employment and contribute to your household needs. Living under the expenses of your relatives or even your parents, at this age isn't fair. This parasite attitude must end and you must find a way to contribute to your household needs," he advised as they all nodded in agreement.

As they dispersed, he walked away hoping today's youths had the passion and perseverance the past generations had, resulting in his small island's recognition for the intellects they once produced. That small island, just the size of three soccer fields produced educated intellectuals such as teachers, doctors, engineers and many more and wondered if anything can be done to bring today's generation to emulate what happened in the past.

With the directions given by Teitione, they found Telanito's uncle, Parani, at a construction site. A construction foreman, he stood with his folders in hand, giving instructions to his workers. Telanito was so proud to see that his uncle was a man of great stature in his organisation.

After being directed by a guard to the boys, Telanito handed him his box - to his delight. He opened the box and took out a large fish and began eating it.

"Uncle, would you be able to find me a job here?" Telanito asked, hoping that his uncle would do him a favour by finding him a job. He often heard stories of people finding employment through wantok system and he wished his uncle, out of pity for his wellbeing in the city, would provide him a job. "I'm sorry my son. We have no vacancies here. Look around, I'm sure you'll find something," responded Parani as he munched on his fish. "See you later. I need to get back to work."

Telakitahuri's next three days in Toniva were spent playing with his nephews on the beach and spoiling them with ice-cream, cookies and toys from the nearby shops. When they were at school, he helped his friend with his job search.

Their job search took them all over the city and, eventually, Telanito was offered a job as a dishwasher at the mine's mess. He was satisfied with the job offered and was asked to return in four days' time - an arrangement perfect to await his friend's departure. As they walked out of his soon-to-be workplace, he thanked Telakitahuri for his assistance.

The evening before Telakitahuri's departure, Teitione and Sione organised a farewell party for him. Telakitahuri and Telanito were playing soccer with the kids when Teitione and Sione arrived with all the food that was needed for the evening's gathering.

Immediately the boys set up the barbecue stand and griller on the lawn and began helping with the preparations. By 4:30 pm, the islanders who resided around Toniva, Kieta and Arawa arrived in numbers. It was usual for Nukutapuans who loved every opportunity to be around each other to share stories and jokes, while the women, especially, liked to show off their recipes of local Nukutapu food. It was their way of showing how much knowledge they had received from their mothers. A variety of food, a typical Nukutapu way, no matter the triviality of the gathering, were spread out on the tables. The islanders loved their seafood which were in abundance, either cooked into different dishes or as fresh as it could be from the sea.

A canvas was spread on the lawn and mothers and children sat on it. The men sat around the spread canvas on chairs and benches while the young boys and girls ran around attending to everyone's needs and, at the same time, giving the cooking mothers a helping hand.

Mokmok stood up and signalled to three other young men. They quickly gathered around a table for a card game of Estimate.

"Put those cards away," Telanito shouted, drawing everyone's attention to Mokmok and his friends. "Don't spoil my friend's party. Mokmok, you often fight over those card games like little kids. So quit it."

The men quickly stopped, cursing Telanito under their breath. They wished no one was around so that they could teach Telanito a lesson. Knowing that, Telanito kept his distance.

Then the low island music was replayed, and almost drowned by the resuming voices of talking and laughing of all those there.

Something caught Telakitahuri's attention. There, in attendance, were people from other cultural groups who were now part of his society through marriage. Some of them even spoke the language and he was amazed. He could see Bougainvilleans, Papua New Guineans, Solomon Islanders and of course, white Lakepas. He wondered how far the Nukutapu gene had spread.

Sione and his wife stood next to the rows of tables of food calling for everyone's attention. They welcomed everyone and Sione gave a short speech about the purpose of the gathering and then welcomed the Member for Atolls, who was also in attendance, and invited him to make a speech.

He stood up, fastened properly his belted floral laplap and joined the two in front. "For all these years, I haven't stopped praising the man above for this inspiration to create this scholarship program for our children. It was very fortunate that the New Zealand ambassador shared my vision and agreed to take it to his government for approval.

"Since its inception, we are blessed to have recipients like Telakitahuri and others, complete their studies and return to contribute in addressing issues affecting our communities on the islands. Climate change, unemployment, high rates of dropouts from school, abuse of substances, lifestyle diseases and many more are threatening the lives of our people.

"So, I not only wish you the best in your final year, I appeal to you, Telakitahuri, to return and be an agent of change for your people," the Member called into the silence that filled that night and everyone roared into cheers when he ended.

The Member's speech challenged Telakitahuri. Being young and naïve, it was a challenge he wasn't prepared to take on. The attractions of the city lights of New Zealand, and Prudence made him choose his words carefully.

"My word of appreciation and thanks to all of you who have turned up. I'm challenged by your expectations on me. Whatever fate brings, I'm hopeful that it will positively impact our community," he managed to say.

After thanksgiving was offered, the women began serving the food. Then the munching, mincing, chomping and clattering began.

As usual, nothing goes wrong with your appetite when a Nukutapuan woman put her magical touch to the food. As everyone waited for dessert, the voice of an intoxicated man raised above the roar of voices from those in attendance.

"Let's sing a lani," called out Tamatai, a retired ship captain whose introversion had been kicked out by a few glasses of iceon the-rock he had while the others ate. In his hay day, he called himself the Devil of the Sea, for his love of being a seaman.

Reluctantly, they all followed his lead of a melodious tune. Back on the island those songs were the islanders' favourite at all occasions. Soon glasses of the best the local lager shops could offer were passed around to make the singing livelier and euphonious.

After singing for some time, Tekosi brought a stick and a 20-litre plastic bottle. Boys and men quickly lined up in front of Tamatai and the other elders as they began their singing and dancing of the traditional dance known as rue.

The singing and dancing continued for some time. The dancers danced as if they were competing with each other. Their ability to manoeuvre to the dance of each song and their stamina to do so were their way of expressing that pride they had for their culture.

"Please put on some music and we'll have a disco instead. Some of us no longer can rue," Parani protested. His lack of association with the islanders had made him forget many of the 15 traditional dances that he had been taught growing up on the island. Many like him often turned up only to find that they had lost a significant part of their lives.

"Stand at the back and follow," called Tekosi. "That is how you get to recall what you have lost."

The dancing went on till late in the night. Slowly Sione rose up to his feet and announced that it was time to end the party.

As vehicles were taking everyone home, Telakitahuri thanked his sister and her husband for hosting a wonderful farewell party for him. Everything he saw about the event was amazing. There was love and unity among the people of Nukutoa. No matter how many years some of them hadn't returned home or had married spouses of other races, their desire to be recognised as Nukutoans was far greater than he had expected. He hoped that it would continue to be like that forever.

Then he and Telanito took a guitar and glasses of wine and sat at the beach. They sang some hulas till it was time to go to bed.

Leaving his loved ones at the Aropa International Airport was heartbreaking for Telakitahuri. As his plane taxied on the runway and glided through the air, he looked down at this beautiful young nation and took pleasure in the wonderful sight that was passing him at a fast pace.

There were great structures that almost matched foreign lands that he'd set foot on. The signs of economic growth were visible from the air. Smoke billowed from the chimneys of production plants and the goodbye waving of the Bougainville flag outside government offices and schools indicated enormous progress in Bougainville's nationhood.

The spectacular scene that he beheld also was the colony of ants crawling about with backs sparkling in reflection in the sun as they went in and out of their queen's abode.

Beyond that, stretched to the south and north, were neatly rowed coconut and cocoa plantations that indicated that agriculture too had its share of contribution to the growth in the Bougainville economy.

The trip was long.

Although his mind was filled with excitement of seeing his course mates and campus friends, his father's face was plastered on everything he thought of. For the past years he hadn't felt that way and he began to worry. He closed his eyes and took a long nap.

The usual scene at Wellington International Airport came to a reality as he descended from the Bougair Boeing 787 and headed to the arrivals hall. The place was packed to capacity with passengers travelling in from all over the world. Their flight also carried many passengers, half of them disembarking at the destination while the others transited to states in Australia. Most of them were tourists who'd spent Christmas and New Year holidaying around Bougainville.

After going through the formal airport checks, he approached the bus station to check his ride, which he had booked online. His ride was all set to go and soon he was covering the 140 kilometers to the campus. The two and a half hours ride was going to be long so he put on his headphones, listened to island music, closed his eyes and fell back into his seat. At that moment, what he needed was a good rest.

But an overwhelming feeling of uncertainty clouded his mind. The joy of returning to his studies, the ambiguity of his father's farewell, and making the choice between Prudence and Tukala were all playing in his mind.

The latter was complicated and his heart was perhaps too weak to address it once and for all. Prudence, a beautiful Business Management student who was lakepa, had completely swooped him off his feet for the last past few years. Her love, kindness, compassion and sense of humour had led to a strong attachment to her.

And Tukala, a village girl whom he had had affections for since they were little, continued to torment his heart with her simplicity every time he saw her. The relationship with her was born of a chemistry that had had its spell over them since they were little. Over the years, a mutual understanding had been fostered that everything would wait till he completed his studies.

Tukala was an arrogant lover who didn't care if he was true to her. All she knew was that she would stay faithful till the day Telakitahuri married or did not marry her. In their latest encounter on the island, he seemed to lean towards her, knowing he didn't have the audacity to convince Prudence to follow him to Bougainville at the end of their studies as being the only child in her family, she was to inherit her parent's real estate business.

On numerous occasions, Telakitahuri had spent holidays with the family in their Wellington mansion and rural farm in Waikato and had grown to like them. They too liked him equally. "Would it affect both Prudence and I, and our studies?" Telakitahuri thought, about his intention to cool off what's between the two of them. "Or should I just leave everything as it is and let fate decide its course?"

The coast bus pulled up in front of the UniLodge Stafford House. The very helpful staff members attended to him and he soon arrived at the comfort of his room. He threw his stuff on the floor, fell onto the bed and slept like a baby in his cradle. When he opened his eyes, he quickly checked the time on his mobile phone. It was 4 p.m. and he'd been asleep for 3 hours.

There were several missed calls registered on his phone: one from his sister and the rest from Prudence. He quickly sent a text message to his sister telling her that he had arrived safely and would call when he'd rested well. He returned the phone to the table and went back to sleep.

Telakitahuri was awoken by loud knocking on the door. He jumped out of bed, and with eyes still sleepy, he opened the door. Standing in front of him was Prudence, obviously angry at his non response to her numerous calls.

"Oh my gosh! What's up with you? I've been calling to no response," she said trying to hide her disappointment.

"I was so tired and took a nap as soon as I arrived. I'm sorry," he apologised as he hugged her. Her fragrance and warmth overwhelmed him and immediately he felt how he longed for her. His mind went crazy, contemplating his desire for her and the idea to put their relationship on halt.

Prudence knew he would arrive that day and had made reservations for them to dine out with her parents in one of the best restaurants not too far from campus. After getting ready they drove off.

Telakitahuri said very little as they drove. "How was home?" she asked interrupting the silence, as she glanced at him. "I almost decided not to return to New Zealand," he quipped, sizing up his girlfriend to see what her reaction would be.

"You must be kidding me!" she exclaimed, turning to look him in the eyes. Her angelic face had deadly eyes that froze to its original elegance of beauty as soon as Telakitahuri broke into great laughter. "You know I'd come looking for you if you hadn't shown your face here," she said in a serious voice.

No more words came out of Telakitahuri's mouth as his mind raced back to what he had thought about that morning. Hearing her words meant things would get nasty should he be forthright with that proposal that he needed space to be alone so that he can deal with his issues. Given that their studies were to commence on Monday, three days away, he needed no major drama to disturb his mind.

Also, sitting beside her, made him feel she's still part of his heart. Prudence's parents were looking at the menu when they walked in. They were so glad to see Telakitahuri again. After shaking hands and hugging, they settled down to place their orders. They had a variety of beverages of their choice as they waited for the food to arrive.

"Telaki, tell Mum and Dad about your visit home," said Prudence, blooming with joy. "Really?" he asked, not knowing if they'd be interested to hear anything about his home. "Off course, we'd love to hear," cried Prudence's mom. "I remember you told me your island was badly affected by the rising sea level. What's your latest assessment of things there?"

Although he wasn't in the mood to talk about home, he had to say something to his hosts. "Although life on the island is amazingly wonderful, I can't say seeing its dire state of ruin due to the effects of climate change is anything my heart can afford to see," he said shaking his head in disgust. "I was born in a hut not too far from the sea, grew up loving everything about it and just can't fathom how something that I've grown to love would be the cause of my people's demise as a race on the face of the earth."

Not only Prudence, but her parents too were touched by Telakitahuri's articulation of the situation on the island. They could hear it all in his voice. "I'm sorry, my dear," whispered Prudence's mother in her most comforting voice. "I wish something could be done to save your home for your future generations."

"Please let not these stories spoil our night," he said trying to sound happy. "I know everything will be all right," said Prudence as she rubbed Telakitahuri's back as a way of comforting him. She knew he was just back from his home and was probably homesick. Their dishes of lobster thermidor were finally laid out on the table.

It was the family's favourite dish, and on every occasion that he'd dined with them, the dish was something they all preferred.

Although he loved the dish, nothing beats a coconut creamed lobster.

He recalled, when he was still in primary school, he and his friends would catch about twenty lobsters. But, before they took their catch home, they would have their own little feast wherever they were. The type of preparation depended on whether they had brought a cooking pot along. If there was a pot, they would have lobster in coconut cream and if no pot was available, it would be roasted lobsters.

After their meal, they sipped their glasses of wine as they chatted. "I have been a keen follower of the Bougainville struggle for independence. It all started when Paul, my brother, travelled to the island as part of the New Zealand Peace Monitoring Team. He wrote me wonderful letters of his stay there. When he returned, he spoke highly of the people and place. One day he told me that Bougainvilleans are intelligent and brave and believed they would achieve their independence."

"And where is he now?" cut in Telakitahuri, eager to meet him if he was around.

"Sadly, his life was taken when he went on another Peace Keeping duty to another foreign country," he sadly said, then turned the conversation to something else.

After their dinner, Telakitahuri asked to be driven back to his room. He said he needed to rest well after the long journey. But Prudence had other ideas. She suggested they spend the weekend either at her family's mansion or book a room at a hotel in Wellington.

After thinking over her suggestions, he insisted he needed to return to his room. Obviously not pleased with Telakitahuri's insistence to be alone, she dropped him off. "I'm just not sure what's got into you. I hope there's nothing serious that you need to tell me," she finally aired her disappointment.

"Darling, there's nothing serious that you need to be alarmed about. I just need a good rest alone so that I'm over this fatigue. Give me Saturday and on Sunday we'll see where we can relax before we commence our studies on Monday," he said trying to dismiss any ill conclusion or doubt that she might have about him.

"Well then, see you on Sunday," she responded calmly. "Do call if you have a change of plan."

As Prudence drove off, Telakitahuri wondered if he had made the right decision. Since their relationship began, they had been inseparable and he knew she could be affected by his decision to be alone. He slumped onto a bench, drew out his phone and dialled his sister's number. The family was glad to hear from him.

He apologised for not calling earlier. Although his sister knew about his relationship with Prudence, she knew that she was not allowed to ask. Their culture tabooed a brother and sister from discussing certain aspects of their lives, and a romantic relationship was one. Just as their conversation was coming to an end, he thought about Telanito.

"By the way, where is Telanito? Can I speak to him?" he asked. "I'm sorry, your friend went to work today and returned at his lunch break to pick up his stuff. His shifts required him to be on site therefore he was provided accommodation," apologised his sister.

"He got your number and said he'd call as soon as he bought himself a phone."

"Oh, I'm so happy for him. I'll wait then for his call," he said. The conversations ended with a goodbye to his cheerful nephews who always loved to hear from him.

Sighing in relief, he stood up and walked to his room. Some students were still outside their rooms, chatting with each other, on their phones, taking their clothes to the laundry and other activities that required them to be outside at that time. He entered his room, put on the TV and searched the channels for Sankamap TV.

The week's segment of People and Places in Bougainville was being telecast. The focus was on the impact of the rising seas on the Nuguria people. His heart broke at the scenes displayed as they were exactly similar to the problems faced by his people back on the island.

As shown, salinisation or the intrusion of seawater through the soil, shoreline erosion and other problems were exactly what his island was facing. The program ended and it was time for the News.

"Good evening viewers, I'm Latu Kiohin, Presenting tonight's news. President pleased with the Economy's Growth, Symposium hosted by the Education Department to discuss relevance of curriculum used in schools. But to begin, the Minister for Climate Change has expressed his concern about the well-being of communities in Bougainville who continue to be affected by climate change, especially the people of the Atolls. He said his department is working with those communities to address pressing issues that have been affecting them. He appealed to donor organisations and NGOs to make their assistance to these communities more impactful than just giving something for the sake of being seen to be offering something."

"For goodness' sake! Come true with your efforts. You seem to be talking too much with very little done. Get real. Our islands are almost gone and you are still blabbering. Take the lead in engaging these donors in real development. You windbag!" he uttered loudly as if the TV set could hear him.

The TV was still on when Telakitahuri woke up on the sofa. He looked at the wall clock: 7:10 a.m. "What are some of the things I need to do before Monday?" he thought to himself.

He remembered that he had given most of his clothes to his father and relatives back in the village. Picking up his mobile phone, he turned on the Note application and began listing all the things that he needed to buy. He put down the mobile phone and headed for the shower. After changing, not even thinking about having a cup of coffee, he locked his room and walked to the bus station.

"Hi Telaki, what's the rush? To catch up with Prudence?" asked Mel, one of Prudence's many friends that he knew very well. "Hi Mel, nice to see you. I'm just off to shop for some clothes," he responded passing her towards the bus station. "See you later," she responded.

Not even a minute passed, when Telakitahuri's phone vibrated. Bringing it to his ear, he could hear Prudence asking where he was off to. He turned back and Mel was out of sight. He knew she was the one who notified Prudence that he was off somewhere. He explained that he needed to get some stuff from the shop.

"Stand right where you are! I'm on my way," her angry voice echoed through the mobile phone. Telakitahuri hated going shopping with her. She would want to buy him this and that and they used to take a long time shopping. He wanted to be as quick as he could.

Not long afterwards, Prudence pulled up. A look at her and Telakitahuri noticed that she was just out of bed and didn't have the time to look at the mirror.

"What happened to all the good clothes you had?" she almost yelled at him.

"I shared them with relatives back home," he reluctantly responded, not too sure what her response would be.

"Oh, that was nice of you. You have a good heart for your

people," she commented. "You could have told me that yesterday."

"Didn't want to bother you," he said calmly. "You know how I hated going shopping with you."

"Don't want to bother me? What is that? I am not leaving you alone! No more!" she told him sternly.

"By the way, you look pretty with no make-up on. I come from a society where make-up isn't in our vocabulary. I love to see that natural beauty in you," Telakitahuri said with a peck on Prudence's cheek.

Then there was complete silence as they drove. Prudence trying to concentrate on the traffic, while Telakitahuri kept his silence knowing Prudence was now fed up with his change of attitude since his arrival. He knew she was suspecting he had been up to some mischief.

Eventually they were at the Fashion Shop. As they stepped out of the car, she asked him what he needed to buy. He showed her the list he had made in his phone. This time the shopping was fast. Prudence needed no approval from him as she threw whatever she felt fitted him into the cart. As she stood waiting for her turn in the queue, Telakitahuri was busy going through the items and removing whatever he didn't want.

It was completely a new wardrobe. They emerged from the shop with Telakitahuri complaining about Prudence's unwise spending and Prudence walking as if she'd lost her hearing.

They drove to the nearby snack bar, ordered some food and headed to watch a game of footy at the park. It was a great day as the two immersed themselves in each other's company. It was the perfect outing that they both needed.

And when Monday arrived, Telakitahuri's final year was truly under way. He woke up early, and though the cold Wellington morning brought shivers, he steeled himself against it and settled into his first lecture of the year. As usual, he took great interest in his studies.

Certain courses intrigued him and he took them very seriously. With his developing interest in assisting his people back home in whatever capacity that he may choose to, he envisioned how his courses could build that knowledge base necessary.

One of those courses was Climate Change Management and Planning. Reflecting on his reasons to take the Bachelor in Development Studies, he said to himself what a coincidence it was. His interest emanated from the fact that Bougainville was a young nation that was going through a lot of development and, by being educated in that field, his expertise will be required.

After his last class of the day, he was too exhausted for Prudence's suggestion for some minutes together. He lay down on his bed and read through his lecture notes and he referred to the many online sources that were cited by the lecturers.

It was their fourth week of study when their lecturer, Professor Radra took them through a study of how certain countries managed disasters that affected them. It was a remarkable study as it enhanced his understanding of why it was vitally important to plan a quick response to disasters, disaster prevention techniques, management of the impacts of various disasters and building community resilience to climate change. With every lesson, he mentally applied that newfound knowledge to the situation on his island.

Telakitahuri and Prudence were sipping coffee one evening as he was looking at his course notes. She popped up with the most unthinkable question that had him struggling for an answer.

"Could these management ideas be applicable should your home encounter a disaster of a large magnitude?" she asked. There was a minute of silence. It wasn't that he couldn't give a response. It was the notion that that idea should never exist that made it hard to respond.

Finally, he spoke. "I know that will never happen. But if it does, applicable strategies will be formulated so that the whole situation can be managed, preventing loss of lives," he answered.

"I'm sorry to ask," she said apologetically as she hugged him and he cuddled her as an acceptance of her apology.

They were just about to disperse for the night's rest when Telakitahuri asked if he could use Prudence's car to make a quick trip to the nearest Western Union agent the next day.

"What's your business there? Is someone sending you money?" asked Prudence, determined to know. "I've seen you go there on several occasion. Do you need money? Why aren't you telling me this?"

The questions kept coming and Telakitahuri was reluctant to say anything. Prudence dropped her folders of papers on the table and sat back on the sofa. "Now, you tell me what I need to know!" she demanded. Finally, he reluctantly explained that he sends part of his allowance to his father back home.

She looked at him in disbelief. She hadn't bothered asking how much allowance he received under his scholarship. But she knew it was a small amount - just enough to keep him going each week.

"We've been together for four years and you have hardly asked me for money or sought my assistance in any way," she said accusingly.

"We are both students, yet to earn a dollar. And remember, we aren't a wedded couple to bother each other with all the problems we have," he warned, not wanting Prudence to be involved in his personal affairs.

However, that was not how Prudence felt about things between them. "We are bound by the love between us. Wedded or not wedded, it is love that makes your problems mine and my problems yours. Who says a ring on my finger should influence the way I should love?" Prudence expressed, as her heart melted by Telakitahuri's act of compassion for his people back home, but couldn't understand how he managed to do it on a student allowance.

Pretending to be cool, she told him she would call in the morning to inform him whether she would drive him there or he could take the car and go by himself.

"By the way, have you spoken to your sister lately?" she asked in great delight, just to cheer him up.

"Oh yes. We spoke over the weekend. Little nephews wanted to speak to me so they called on Saturday evening," he responded, happy to talk about them.

"I remember how surprised she was when I answered her call last year. Do you recall that?" she asked with a giggle.

"Off course! You made her think she had called a wrong number. She's cool with that," he said with a smile on his face.

"I'd love to speak to her one day if you don't mind," she uttered looking into his face as if begging for the response she wanted.

"Not at all. Here's her number," he said as he read out her number and Prudence scribbled it on her notebook.

Soon Prudence was on her way to her room. She too had a room on campus, but occasionally she returned to her family home not too far away, when she wanted to.

As she drove, she laughed to herself at the thought of Telakitahuri falling into her trap. As for Telakitahuri, he didn't know if he had made the right decision to give Teitione's number to Prudence.

The early winter morning did not deter Telakitahuri from rising up to meet another day of intense learning. He sipped his coffee as he looked at his timetable for the day. Beside 11 a.m., when he had no classes, he wrote 'Western Union'.

Unknown to him that at that very moment, Prudence was having a long conversation with Teitione. She introduced herself as Telaki's girlfriend and the two had a long conversation. Before ending, Prudence promised to notify her as soon as she's made the transfer for the old man. She told her to notify Telaki by text message as soon as she'd made the withdrawal. She then called her company accounts and ordered a transfer through Western Union to the details that she would forward shortly.

At 11 a.m. Telakitahuri exited the lecture hall heading out to see if he could make the trip to the agent. It was time to make his transfer to his sister. As he found his way through the many students, he remembered he did not receive a good response from Prudence about the use of her car. Pulling out his phone and switching it on as it had been off since morning, a message popped up. It was from his sister.

"What now?" he sighed as he opened the message, and to his amazement, it read, "Thanks. Have made the withdrawal and deposit into father's account."

"No. No. No. I haven't made the transfer. How could she possibly say that," he cried.

Then a thought came into his mind. "Prudence!" he exclaimed.

He shook his head as he hurried along the path leading to her course lecture rooms. He dialled her number. But her phone was off. Entering the building, he darted straight for the door of her lecture room. He pulled the door but it was locked. Peering through the glass section of the door, there she was, innocently concentrating on her lecture. He moved to the side, put his head against the wall and let out a few soft sobs.

The feeling was overwhelming. Composing himself, he slowly walked out, heading towards his residential hall. He needed to talk to his sister and perhaps a short nap to get over this. After making himself comfortable on his bed, he pulled out his mobile phone and dialled his sister's number.

"Hello. Teaso tokoreka," came her sister's voice, animatedly lively. "Hello, good day," he responded and then the conversation began with all laughter about the situation. He told her he was taken by surprise by her text message and the noises she made, told him she was laughing. Then she told him about Prudence's call and that made sense of everything. He gave a big laugh and her sister also burst into laughter.

"I didn't want her to be involved with my family. But you know, she's something else," he said with more accolades for Prudence. "But don't you say a word about her to anyone. You know how our islanders can be at times."

"I know," his sister assured him. Telakitahuri was relieved after all. All he needed to do now was thank his love for her act of kindness. He took his nap and woke up just in time to return for his next lecture. As he picked himself up to head to the lecture room, he felt a sense of longing for Prudence's presence. What he felt when he first arrived was no longer there. The lecture seemed to be the longest, as he hoped that it would end sooner. It was one of the courses that he loved. However, that did not make sense at that moment because he had something else on his mind.

Back on the island, bad weather had confined everyone to their homes for about a week. Catching fish had been difficult and those with money were the lucky ones who could afford a canned protein from the trade stores. The little money Telakitahuri had given his dad had run out and he was now waiting on his son's promise of some more money. Although Teitione had called several times, she hadn't sent anything based on Telakitahuri's instructions.

Her call today sounded different. She was full of life. "How are you, tamana?" asked Teitione.

"I'm all right. It's just that the weather here is very bad and I'm desperate for a cup of coffee and maybe a meal of Ox&Palm would make my afternoon." said the old man, expecting a bit of a pity from his daughter.

"Well then go and get them," she said. "Your son sent you money. Hello. Hello." The line was dead and Teitione had to redial. The old man came on again. She asked him what happened to his phone. "Bad reception," he lied, smiling to himself at his mishap in the excitement of receiving the wonderful message from her daughter. In his haste to remove his bank card from the side pocket of his phone cover, he had disengaged the call accidently.

After their call, the old man entered the trade store. He made his purchase of all he wanted, took out some cash and swung his shopping as he whistled on his way home. He saw some young girls including Tukala sitting on the beach braiding their hair. Tukala was as pretty as she could be with her long hair all straightened to be braided. Pride overwhelmed him as he detoured for a route that passed them by few metres.

The gossips he had heard about the two's involvement made him proud of his son's preference of beauty.

"Hi girls, my son sent me some money so I went to collect a few things," he unashamedly announced. "Would you want something sweet from the store?"

"That's kind of you to ask. We are all right," Tukala responded to the protest of the other girls.

"I insist," he said as he offered one of the girls the money. He swung his shopping as he whistled along his way. In his lucky days, his generosity clouded all his ideas of what suffering meant.

The day's classes came to an end and Telakitahuri and his course mates emerged from their lecture room continuing the discussion they had in their lesson as they walked. Suddenly his phone rang and he excused himself to take the call.

"You've got some explanations to make," he said into the mouth piece of the device. He could hear her giggling at the other end.

"Where are you?" she asked.

"I'm on my way out. Wait for me at the car park," he said.

That night was a whole new experience for the two. They rekindled their love and expressed their love for each other. There were no books, biros, mobile phones as the two sat chatting in Prudence's room.

"I got a text message from Teitione saying that the old man was overjoyed," said Telakitahuri, his face lighting up with joy. "It was just as they were experiencing bad weather that prevented anyone from going fishing. He was dying for some protein when Teitione called."

"My goodness, I can't wait for us getting out of this place, have a house of our own and get him here," pitied Prudence.

"I doubt that will happen. He doesn't even want to join Teitione in Toniva," he said shaking his head. It was getting towards the end of their school calendar and Telakitahuri was so busy with his studies. Lectures, tutorial classes, 29 assignments and tests all kept him busy. Final year and the workload was hectic.

Like him, Prudence too was experiencing her share of the load and they only met during the weekends to spend time together.

It was on a Friday afternoon, late spring, when they decided to venture out to the coast to take a weekend to relax. They loaded Prudence's car with what they needed and they headed to Oriental beach where they booked a bungalow for the weekend. Their plan was to free their minds from all that was going on at campus and, at the same time, quietly work on their assignments.

As they got out of the car to get to their bungalow, Telakitahuri could not take his eyes off the sea. It was like he had seen an ex-girlfriend whom he still loved and hadn't seen in ages. His mind raced back to his island and there was satisfaction that he had made the choice to be there.

After inspecting everything in their new home for the weekend, they ventured to the seashore. There were lots of people on the beach. Telakitahuri walked into the sea to get a feel of it while Prudence was busy with her camera.

"Let's take a selfie," shouted Prudence as Telakitahuri was about to dive into the water. "No. No. Take off your clothes first."

Telakitahuri returned to Prudence who was ready with her camera, not to take a selfie but to take off his long pants and shirt. As he took them off, she sat beside him taking her shots. He knew she would post them on social media and put up funny faces to a protesting Prudence.

He was about to leave for the water when he realised he had left his phone on the sand. Picking it up, he took a selfie of himself with the sea at the background. He was about to tag his friends and an idea came into his mind. His poetic mind came into play as his fingers played around with the keyboard of his phone.

"Silly me!" he gasped in hesitation, contemplating whether to delete or continue. His customary laws forbade the utterance of explicit language which can be seen or heard by his sisters or cousin sisters. It may be deemed disrespectful. However, he could not brush aside this sense of connection he had with the sea and he felt that was the best possible way he could express his feelings. Thus he continued.

*She's calm and charming*

*I gasped lovingly at her beauty,*

*that wonderfully stretched out.*

*I watched her moves.*

*Soft undulations seductive and inviting.*

*My heart beats with lust*

*I dare take her and loomed closer*

*Her briny aroma overwhelming*

*I'm now under her spell*

*Longing for her*

*To cool this burning heat.*

*Stripping to my core,*

*I drew nearer*

*Eyeing the animated life in her*

*Overcome with sensation*

*And wasting no time*

*I splashed into her coolness*

*Mesmerised by her cuddle*

*Of gentle caressing touches*

*I succumb to her wholeness.*

*As I breathe a sigh of relief*

*I came out all wet,*

*And stood on the beach,*

*Looking at her.*

*In spite of this love,*

*I cursed her,*

*Under my salty breath.*

*For her rages of madness,*

*Was shredding my island,*

*Into unreturnable fragments,*

*That may send me packing,*

*For my refuge.*

"What are you doing?" asked Prudence, peering to see what has been keeping him busy.

In deep thought, he had been typing on his phone and she was wondering what he was doing. Curiosity took the better of her and she maneuvered around him to take a look.

She held his hand still and as she perused the first lines, she uttered, "Is it about me?" The gleeful smile that spread across her face vanished as soon as she understood what it was.

"Sorry my dear," he apologised not even taking an eye off the screen of his mobile. "Let me put the last touch and then I'll explain." After some minutes, he gave a sigh of relief and turned to her and explained what the poem was about.

"Wonderful! You sure have a creative mind," she marvelled. "You have personified your subject very well. Go ahead and post it."

Telakitahuri posted it and they both ran off into the sea. They had a great time in the water just like all those who were there that afternoon until Prudence decided it was time to return to their bungalow. It was the best weekend he had had for a long time.

Late in the night he sat on the balcony and watched the waves roll up and down the beach. It reminded him of his home. On his trip there he noticed that the beach was no longer sandy. Instead, rocks had appeared. It was once his favourite playground. Every morning before they bathe to go to school, they would play a variety of games till their mothers would come chasing them all to hurry them to school. The afternoon baths weren't different. They would play until they could no longer see each other in the dark.

"My dear, come in. It's getting late," called Prudence, who was busy working on her laptop.

"Coming," he responded. Saturday and Sunday were spent relaxing on the beach and perusing their course material on their iPads, chatting, cuddling on the sand, swimming and strolling along the beach. It was a perfect weekend away from the weekend activities on campus.

By Sunday 2 p.m. they were all packed, ready to return to campus when Teitione called. She told Telakitahuri that she had had a conversation with the old man and things weren't looking good. Hearing that, he abruptly ended the call by turning the phone off, preferring to calm himself before he could continue the conversation.

At this time, he had no clear understanding of what she meant by what she said. As they were about to drive off, he composed himself and begged that they hurry back to the campus.

"What did she say?" Prudence asked, as she accelerated. She began to be concerned by Telakitahuri's high level of anxiety and stress. His eyes were watery and he uttered very little as they drove.

"Don't know. I'll confirm as soon as we arrive," he said in almost a whisper.

His phone lay off on the dashboard. "Is your phone out of power? Here, charge it and call her back," she demanded, getting anxious at every minute of Telakitahuri's self-imposed silence.

"Don't worry, I'll do that as soon as we reach the campus," he responded calmly.

Although the car engine was roaring, the silence of no utterances from either of them was deafening, especially for Prudence. She was uneasy about the situation Telakitahuri was in, but could not draw him into a conversation. She was confused as to whether Telakitahuri would want a conversation or remain quiet.

Finally, they pulled up at the parking area outside his residence. Prudence got out and she started taking his stuff into his room while he stood outside the car switching his phone on. The network came on and text messages flooded in. One message notification indicated that he had missed calls from Teitione.

He opened the first message, which read "Nukutapu on alert. Tidal waves hitting the island from northern side." He froze in fear. Just then, a text came in and it read, "Check Nukutapu Facebook page. Things not looking good." It was from Telanito.

"How serious is that?" he said to himself as he opened Facebook to the Nukutapu page. The scenes captured in the photographs and videos were too much for him to handle. In a split of a second, his world came crumbling down. He wanted to scream. But nothing came out and darkness befell him.

"Help! Help! Somebody help call an ambulance," cried Prudence as she raced to Telakitahuri's motionless body on the pavement. She picked up his upper body and laid him on her lap. Gently raising his face towards her, fear overwhelmed her. His eyes were all white and saliva drooled out from the corners of his mouth. Her body began to shiver in fear. It was an experience she hadn't had in her whole life.

A student called the ambulance, while the others rushed in to offer whatever help they could. For some minutes they tried to revive him with whatever First Aid knowledge they had. However, he remained unresponsive. Someone rushed in with a bottle and poured water on his head and in an instant, he came back to his senses.

He opened his eyes and was surprised to find himself in the hands of all those trying to resuscitate him. And there was Prudence wailing as if he was gone, dead. She saw his open eyes and stopped crying, cuddling his face into her chest as she whispered, "You'll be all right, love."

Just then the wailing siren of the ambulance arrived. The paramedics raced out to attend to him. He was in a state of shock and remained unresponsive to their questions. They lifted him up and walked him into the ambulance. A paramedic looked at him and commented that he looked stressed.

Prudence knew he wouldn't speak so she told the paramedics what had happened to him. "Sir, his condition deteriorated after receiving some news of a natural disaster that happened at his home," explained Prudence as Telakitahuri sat listening.

His senses returned and he lay back on the bed and began to cry. The paramedic ordered Prudence in, shut the door and they drove off. Arriving at the hospital, Telakitahuri was taken to a room. The psychiatrist assessed his vitals and instructed him to take a rest on a bed. He got onto the bed, closed his eyes and rested.

Prudence stood on the side and watched him. Her heart broke as she watched tears slipping from his closed eyes, each one a silent story of sorrow. "Be strong, my man," she whispered into his ear. Not wanting to disturb him, she took her phone and exited the room.

Looking through the glass door at the sleeping Telakitahuri, she dialled Teitione's number.

A voice drowned by emotions responded in a manner it took a moment to comprehend. The voice summed up the situation at hand and Prudence knew it was serious. As she listened to Teitione, the missing pieces in Telakitahuri situation began to fall into place.

"How bad is the damage?" Prudence asked. "Very bad," she responded, holding back sobs that almost choked her. After a short pause she uttered, "The sea had inundated the entire village."

The moment Prudence told her about Telakitahuri, Teitione broke down and, after listening to her wailing, she switched off the phone and returned to Telakitahuri who was then undergoing his second check-up with the psychiatrist.

"Doctor, what is your diagnosis?" she asked.

"I'm not sure what's wrong with him. His vitals seem to be improving. However, he is totally withdrawn," he responded. "Would you know if he or his family have mental health issues?"

As soon as Prudence finished explaining to the doctor what really happened to Telakitahuri, he picked up the phone and called the counsellor to provide the patient with some counselling. Some minutes later, the counsellor walked in. He asked Prudence to leave the room so that he could have a private session with Telakitahuri.

After an hour, the Counsellor opened the door and called Prudence in. "I'm afraid I'll have to monitor his condition for at least another 24 hours. There's a possibility that he might experience a relapse," he explained.

He asked Prudence to follow him into the glassed consulting room and he advised her that the patient's current status required close observation for the next 48 hours as there was a possibility that he could be suicidal if he can't handle what's going on in his mind.

"Counsellor, can you ask the nurse to keep an eye on him while I give my parents a call and collect a few things for our stay here?" asked Prudence in her most polite voice.

"Don't worry. The nurses are here to provide the care necessary and I'll be in and out of here until his condition improves," he responded.

After letting Telakitahuri know, Prudence drove back to pick up the things they would need during their stay at the hospital. As she drove, she called her mother to let her know what had happened to her boyfriend. Her mother was surprised to hear that and promised she and her dad would be there in no time.

Lying on that bed, helpless as he was, tears rolled down the side of Telakitahuri's eyes as the thought of his father and all those on the island, kept playing in his mind. The images he had seen on social media, and his own ideas of how the people on the island would struggle to safety were like a 40-inch screen glued to his face so that, everywhere he looked, those images would come into place, affecting him terribly.

"I need you to take this medicine," said the nurse as she placed a glass of water and a tray of tablets on the table next to his bed. Without delay, he took the medicine and, in a few minutes, he was sound asleep like a baby in its cradle.

Prudence returned to find her parents in the parking lot. A s they walked to the ward, Prudence explained what had happened to Telakitahuri. Their hearts broke when they heard about the ordeal that he had gone through.

They arrived to find him in deep sleep. The nurse explained to them that she had given him some medicine to ease the tension that was building in his mind. She said that when he woke up, he would feel a lot better.

After spending two days in the hospital, Telakitahuri was in a better state to return to campus. The psychiatrist sat him down and went through what he need not do while he was out. It was a list of things that he thought would create a relapse if he wasn't careful.

He told the Counsellor that it was the shock of what happened to his home that caused his mental breakdown and believed nothing serious would recur.

Settling into his apartment, Telakitahuri felt relaxed and relieved to be back. He picked up his phone with the idea of calling his sister. However, Prudence gave him a look that made him change his mind.

He returned the phone to the table and gazed dreamily at the ceiling.

"Listen, I've spoken to Teitione and she wants you not to think too much, as everything is under control," Prudence explained.

"Did you speak to her? Does she know I was in hospital?" persisted Telakitahuri, very concerned that his sister would worry about him.

Prudence explained to him that she had been in contact with her about his condition and the welfare of those in the village.

As she continued, Telakitahuri sat staring into her eyes as if he had found something new in her that he never knew existed.

Not known to Telakitahuri was that his once beautiful island, Nukutapu, was now a thing of the past. Since recovering from the psychological trauma that had affected him when news first reached him, Prudence, through Teitione's advice had restricted his use of his mobile phone. It was she who would speak with Teitione and relay carefully crafted messages that they felt would not affect him.

Weeks had gone past and Telakitahuri sat in his lecture listening to his lecturer talking about Disaster Risk Resolution. He said "DRR is a systematic approach to identifying, assessing and reducing the risk of disaster." That statement hit him.

"Had this approach been considered for the benefit of my people?" he thought to himself, while what could have happened if more reliable prevention methods had been considered for the island. He knew it was a costly exercise and the community and the local government would not have had the expertise and resources unless there was an intervention from NGOs, Donor Countries or the national government.

"Disasters are prone to happen anywhere at any time. It is our ability to foresee that and make educated judgments on how to mitigate those risks that will reduce the impact that they can have on us," added Professor Sing.

The lecture came to a conclusion and Professor Sing asked if anyone had anything to say. Everyone seemed to look forward to lunch and none showed any interest. But Telakitahuri raised his hand and the Professor was glad someone had something to say.

"While we are going through this topic, I'd like to make a statement in relation to my experience of a disaster. Predictable as it was, nothing was done all these years till it came to a time that was, perhaps, too late. My island was recently affected by a disaster that, under the threats of climate change, we knew one fine day it may happen. However, we have been talking about the issue and even resources such as money had been wasted on talking about the issue and nothing had been done to reduce the risk involved. When strong winds and waves hit my island of Nukutapu, there was nothing my people could do except to find ways to survive the ordeal: a very terrible experience my people should not have had to endure. This lecture has taught me a great lesson that once I know that I am prone to disasters, I must be able to identify the kind of disasters that are likely to affect me, assess how they will affect me and find ways to reduce its impact," said Telakitahuri with a voice full of confidence, though emotional.

"A very good statement. Was it your village that was recently inundated by strong tides? I saw it in the news. I'm deeply sorry for that traumatic experience your people went through," said Professor Sing.

"Thank you, Professor. Yes, it was my island. But it was only hit by strong winds and tides that affected part of it," corrected Telakitahuri.

"I may be wrong. But I thought I heard it correctly," asserted the Professor with confidence.

Telakitahuri stormed out of the room. Not that he was hungry like all the other students who were heading straight to the mess to grab a bite. He headed straight to his room, picked up his phone and searched his Dad's number. Something different was burning in him and he wasn't affected like when he first got the news. He thought about calling but wasn't satisfied with only hearing his father's voice. He wanted to see his face and see the actual situation on the island.

He put on his Wi-Fi and opened the application that he used to video call his father. He looked at his status and he was online. A touch on the dial and his father came on live.

The rolling tears down his father's wrinkled, unshaven cheeks broke his heart as he fought the urge to cry. He wanted to be strong for his father.

"Nice to see you again, my son," came the cracking voice that was almost drowned by the sorrow that filled his heart.

"Nice to see you too, Dad. I love you," responded Telakitahuri.

The conversation was emotional as they tried to find comfort in knowing each other's welfare, reassuring each other that everything was all right. His father had learnt from Teitione the trauma he had gone through and was asking a lot of questions about his welfare.

No matter how hard he explained that he was all right, he could see the unconvincing look on his face.

"Where are you now?" asked Telakitahuri, trying to look past his father to have a good look at the background.

"Son, don't you worry. We are now all doing fine on Nukutoa. Nukutapu is now only sand. Everyone has evacuated to Nukutoa," said the old man.

"The professor was right," he thought to himself as he listened to his father. His father told him about their new resettlement and even walked around with the camera on so that he could see everything that he wanted to see.

There were men working on their new houses, women cooking and doing other things to fix up the place and the children playing on the sandy beach.

"Wow, my heart breaks to see you all like that," he uttered after composing himself and finding some courage to say it out loud.

"Don't you worry son. We'll persevere. Complete your studies and see what you can do for your people," said his father.

That was the first time he had heard his father utter such a challenge.

He was a leader in the village but never in his life did he put a responsibility as such on his shoulders.

"All right dad, I heard you. I have to return for my afternoon classes. Let my cousin Lakia know I wish to speak to him in the coming days," he said and then ended their call with some touching goodbyes.

He put down his phone and was about to leave when it vibrated. He looked at the screen and it was Prudence.

"Hello darling," he answered into the mouthpiece of the phone. "What's happening? Your phone's been busy for almost an hour. Who were you online with?" responded Prudence.

"I had a video call with my dad. It seemed there were a lot you and Teitione hid from me. But that's all right. I understand. We'll get through all these issues," he said.

"Let's meet after lectures," she said putting her phone off.

That afternoon, after lectures ended, Telakitahuri threw his stuff on the sofa in his room and headed out to sweat it out on the basketball court. A good number of students, a mixture of males and females, were already there, preparing for a game. They quickly formed their teams and began playing.

He had a wonderful time and, when he spotted Prudence cheering on the sideline, he remembered she wanted them to meet. "Can I have a replacement, please," he called out to those who stood watching.

Someone ran in as he walked off to meet Prudence. "I needed to sweat myself. This cold is making me sick," he said to Prudence as they walked to his room.

"What was your conversation with your dad about?" asked Prudence as Telakitahuri was about to head for his hot shower.

"We had a long conversation. I'll tell you when I'm done here," responded Telakitahuri as he got into his warm bath.

The sprinkling of warm water rejuvenated a new self in him, forcing out a hum of pleasure. He was fresh and ready for anything Prudence suggested. As he eyed himself in the mirror, he asked Prudence what plans she had for them that afternoon.

"I've got no plans. Just wanted to know if you are all right after your conversation with your father. And if you agree, we can send some things on the ship destined to travel to the island," she said.

"I thought so too," he said. "You know my father gave me a challenge today and I am ready to shoulder that challenge starting today. I will not wait till I graduate from here. Big or small, they will all be part of my plans and contributions to the welfare of my people."

"I'm so proud of you. You have a big heart for your people. I believe this passion in you will grow into something in the future," said Prudence, eyeing him admiringly.

After much discussion, everything was all planned out for implementation. Its success depended on how determined Telakitahuri was about fulfilling his father's wishes.

After they kissed each other good night, Telakitahuri watched Prudence's car disappear into the night. He knew he had a strong lady at his back to make all those plans a reality.

On Nukutoa, Lakia woke up early. Not only was it that his sleep wasn't comfortable on the dried coconut leaves that cracked at every turn, but his mind, too, was making its rounds all over the island.

All the work of settling into their new home on Nukutoa had been keeping them busy all day long and his mind was too worried about all the unfinished business' to sleep.

He emerged from the house, squinting. Although the sun was yet to pop its head through the horizon, the little light of the breaking day made him feel like he was developing photopia.

Picking up a bottle of water, he washed his eyes as he walked to the beach. He could see someone sitting on a canoe that was pulled up ashore. He walked closer and the distinct figure of his uncle became clearer. Eyes affixed at the direction of Nukutapu, he sat staring. He was in his own world.

"Good morning Uncle," he said. "Good morning," responded his uncle without even looking to see who he was. He took his eyes from what he was looking at and as he bowed in thought, Lakia could see tears dropping.

Lakia understood what was going through his mind. He sat on the other canoe and for some minutes neither of them uttered a word. The silence overwhelmed them and Lakia began to feel what the old man was going through.

"I've lived 75 years on that island and thousands of years of history have passed through the generations that grew up on that island. Why does it have to happen in my lifetime? Why didn't it just wait till I'm gone?" he said as he shook his head.

"Uncle, I understand what you are going through. But disaster is uncontrollable," comforted Lakia.

"Where were all the Aitus? Didn't they see that the waves were destroying our island? All these times, I believed they were protecting our island," responded the old man putting all blame on the Aitus.

"The God that I believe in says, 'To everything there is a season, a time for every purpose under heavens.' Let's not dwell on what we have lost and work hard to protect what we now have. Nukutoa, under no circumstances, is safe from such disasters. What we did not do on Nukutapu must be done here on Nukutoa. If we talk and talk without action, Nukutoa will go down just like Nukutapu," advised Lakia.

When their conversation about the topic ended, the old man recalled Telakitahuri's intention to speak to Lakia. He quickly took out his tablet from inside the canoe and extended his hand to Lakia. "Here, check if the Wi-Fi is on and your brother is online. He wanted to have a word with you," said the old man.

Lakia was soon waiting for his cousin to answer. The wait wasn't long when Telakitahuri's face appeared on screen. While he was happy to see his cousin, he apologised that he had to end the call and call him later as he was in class.

Without apologising, Lakia abruptly ended the call. "He's already in class!" exclaimed the old man. "Impossible! The sun just rose and how could he be so early to class. That's probably what they do at university: less sleep and learn, learn, and learn."

"No Uncle, I should have sent him a message to call when he's free. We have different time zones that means that if it is 6 am here, it could be 10 am in New Zealand."

"There you go again with your lies and deceits. How could that be possible? In the past, our ancestors travelled the vast oceans from Samoa, Tonga, Hawaii, and even New Zealand and it's the same sun that they saw," said the old man, thinking he was being fooled by Lakia.

Lakia went to the trouble of trying to explain the different time zones to his uncle. The explanation became complicated with the old man refusing to believe in his theory that there were different time zones.

He pulled back the tablet from him and googled time zones. The information popped up and he passed the tablet back to the old man, demanding that he read it. Reading through that, he smiled and then apologised.

"Sorry son, the little education I got just enabled me to read and write. I never took interest in the other things school taught. I was more interested in learning my traditional knowledge. It's a pity that traditional knowledge will pass as our community modernises," he said with mixed thoughts.

What actually troubled him disappeared when his phone chimed indicating a message. He stared at the screen. "Will call in two and a half-hour's time," read the message from Telakitahuri.

The men were putting up the frames of houses with materials cut from the forest while the women weaved coconut leaves for the roofs and walls when the old man's phone rang. Everyone turned to look at the ringing phone. They all have heard of Telakitahuri's scheduled call and were eager to hear what he intended to say to Lakia.

"Get the phone!" called the old man to Lakia. Quickly Lakia ran and picked up the phone. It was the video call from his cousin that they had been expecting.

As the two exchanged their greetings, everyone, from wherever they were, shouted their hellos at Telakitahuri. Lakia quickly turned the camera so that Telakitahuri could see everyone.

As soon as he saw everyone and the houses that they were constructing, tears ran down his eyes. He wept openly and everyone soon surrounded Lakia, urging Telakitahuri not to cry. One by one, they gave him comforting messages. And from time to time, their communication was interrupted by a white hand that wiped away tears from Telakitahuri's eyes.

When all were composed with their sorrows, especially Telakitahuri, a little boy interrupted them. "Uncle, whose hand was that?" he asked to the approval of everyone.

For a second, Telakitahuri's eyes looked up, as if someone was standing behind his gadget. Before Prudence could stop him, she was in the eyes of more than 20 eagerly curious strangers. With nowhere to escape, she said hello to everyone.

When the hype of the moment died down, Lakia asked everyone to move away so that they could speak privately. Everyone followed the old man. As soon as they were a distance away, they started asking the old man all kinds of questions regarding the woman who had appeared in the video on the phone. Concerned at the thought of Telakitahuri marrying a lakepa, he brushed them aside, not wanting it to be a topic of discussion. Tukala was the girl he wanted for his son and he was afraid the gossips would reach her.

Telakitahuri confided to his cousin about his plans. He will be his main man on the ground. He asked him to use the old man's phone to take pictures of their sunken island and all of the activities that were happening on the island.

After saying goodbye to his cousin, he hugged Prudence, satisfied that his plans were beginning to take shape.

Four days after Telakitahuri and Lakia's conversation, Telakitahuri received the pictures that he had requested. Though glad that he'd got the pictures, the scenes were heart breaking. Lakia did not only take photos; he also collected photos and videos of that fateful day. Tears rolled down his eyes as he scrolled down the pictures as Prudence watched from behind.

"That's heartbreaking," she comforted as she tapped his shoulder.

"Sure it is," Telakitahuri managed to utter. "I don't know how much impact the responsibility I am assuming will have on my studies. But I know I will persevere."

Everything they planned to do had been mapped out thoroughly and it was only a matter of execution. As they returned to their afternoon lectures, Telakitahuri felt a surge of confidence and determination that he must act now or never. Ideas would pop up in his mind and he would jot them down. Although his passion for his new ideas was getting stronger, his studies were still his priority.

"I've spoken with my family about assisting you and we believe that for help to flow in, you have to have an organisation in place, not only for recognition purposes, but for others who will be appointed to various roles to help out with some of those responsibilities," advised Prudence as they sat for an evening meal at the campus cafeteria.

"I know. I've been jostling with the idea of flying back. But I really can't afford to do that with the exams just weeks away. Also to leave it to my return after studies end, would derail everything we've planned. I'm a bit confused," responded Telakitahuri with great concern.

"How about a video chat?" cried out Prudence, as she searched for a positive response in Telakitahuri's sorry eyes. "You got it!" exclaimed an elated Telakitahuri. "Though it would be a good idea, I don't know how I can get those on the island to participate. Having more than ten people surrounding one mobile phone wouldn't be ideal for a perfect discussion. I just don't have sufficient funds to send appropriate equipment for that purpose."

The expression on Telakitahuri said it all. And Prudence was not going to let her man down like that. She agreed to help out, amidst Telakitahuri's protest.

After much discussion, everything was agreed upon for execution.

"Call Sione right away and ask him about when the ship will depart for the island," instructed Prudence, feeling the urge to get things sorted as soon as possible.

Telakitahuri picked up his phone. He dialled Sione's number and a raspy hello came alive on the other side, followed by a moment of clearing of his vocal cords. Finally, he was ready to speak. The conversation lasted an hour as Telakitahuri outlined his plans to an absolutely overwhelmed Sione.

"I am so proud of you. Since the disaster, everything seemed to have died down. Conniving men who took the lead in trying to get some assistance for the people suddenly vanished when the government announced that cash was tight and they'll be waiting for outside support," said Sione and proceeded to throw in some ideas.

"What do you think? As soon as we end this conversation, I will send a message for all our people working all over the country to contribute to this initial move to help our people. The government has not been coming good with our people. Therefore, it is only appropriate that we make the move."

"Although I wouldn't push you to do that, I believe every person with Nukutoa blood in their veins must have it in their hearts to give something to their community.

Numerous times, I've heard people saying that they are married out of the island or had been out of the island for a long time and can't be bothered with the island's issues. Yet they continue to identify themselves as from Nukutoa or Mortlock Islander. What happens if there is no longer an island by that name? The last thing we all want is to identify ourselves as being from the Mortlock Ocean," Telakitahuri said as he broke into a chorus of laughter.

On the other side, Sione didn't take his sense of humor well. Through Telakitahuri's eyes, he was beginning to see the danger posed to his Mortlock identity.

"Well then, I will send you the list of things to buy as well as the money. Make sure you get everything ready before the ship sails in two days' time."

The villagers were all at Nukutapu trying to salvage anything they could find in the seas surrounding their former home. Roofing iron, water tanks, cooking utensils and many other household possessions were located and bought to the shallow waters ready to be brought by boats and canoes to Nukutoa.

On that fateful day, it was the canoes and boats that saved their lives. They took whatever belongings they could take and departed the island before the huge waves of tokorau dissected the island into mere sand, inundated by the sea.

Returning to their former home was emotional. Memories of the past emerged with every find they made. Some were lucky to find things of value to themselves, to their family and to their entire clan. Most of what they found were items that could not float. It was indeed a surreal experience.

At 3 in the afternoon, when there was no hope of finding more things, Telakitahuri's father climbed up what was now a sand dune. Sitting down with legs hanging on the edge of the dune, he called out to a young girl to take a photo of him with his tablet that was in a small water-tight bag that was on the boat. He planned to send the photo to his son as soon as he returned to Nukutoa.

The girl admiringly took out the tablet from its cover and took the shot. She returned the tablet to the old man and he stared at the shot. There was a flock of birds at the background resting before their flight to search for food around the lagoon.

He turned and looked at them. He knew that his former home was now a refuge for all kinds of birds. With eyes welling up to the hurt that gripped his heart, in his clearest and loudest voice, he sang, and everyone joined in with their melodious tunes.

*The birds that grew up on the shores,*

*Cried as they flew away.*

*In front of my eyes,*

*They flew away.*

*The birds that laid their eggs on the shores,*

*Had their eggs washed away.*

*In front of my eyes,*

*Their generations are gone.*

*The friendship we shared on those shores,*

*Are now only memories,*

*Scattered like those birds.*

*We took our own flights.*

Their mournful tune went on repeat for a while, only interrupted by a little boy's sudden screams. Everyone looked at the direction of his hand and true, there was MV Tausena manoeuvring through the narrow passage as it made its way into the lagoon.

Loading everything that they'd gathered, the strongest men, with poles in their hands, began to push the boats and canoes while the rest of the people walked the shallow reef through the 10 islands to Nukutoa.

The trip back was full of fun as jokes were shared and songs were sung as they made their way back to their new home, optimistic that some help was finally arriving to alleviate the struggles that they endured since their terrible encounter.

On the ship, Telanito stood at the bow scanning the distance for his beautiful Nukutapu. He had sought permission from his employer to return home to see his family. Never in his life, and it was not only him, but all the islanders who were on the ship, cried like someone had just passed away.

In respect for the people and their sunken island, the captain followed his waypoint to his usual anchorage spot off the shore of the once Nukutapu Island. A boat was lowered and the Chairman of the Nukutapu Community Government and four other men, whose roles were to assess the situation, climbed onto the boat and sped to the dune of sand as the ship altered its course towards Nukutoa Island.

It was a sad reunion for the arrivals. They could not bear to see their families make it out of the bush material houses that they had built. It was such an unforgiving sight that they wished the cause of all that was available for a bashing.

Finally, the chairman arrived to a teary welcome from his people. The whole village was there to hear what he and those who accompanied him had to say.

"Good afternoon everyone. My heart breaks to see our beautiful island gone and you all struggling to get back on your feet. We all don't deserve to be like this. However, nature is something we have no control over. I questioned our creator why this had to happen to us. But I also thank him that, through his mercy, he has delivered us safely out of harm. Out of the vast lands and high mountains, he led our ancestors to this island. For what? So we can be tested for our endurance and durability to survive in such circumstances? But I am sure that he has not forsaken us. If he sent his son to die for our sins, there is no way that he has forsaken us," his speech was interrupted with a thunderous "Amen" from the crowd.

The speeches continued till dusk when Laumana, the ship's chef, led his kitchen hands to deliver boxes of dinner packs. It was a compliment from the ship's management. On the sandy beach, families sat to indulge in their spoils - a meal they hadn't had for some time.

As they ate, Lakia called out for their attention. "Tomorrow, I want all of us to meet here at around 10:00 am. Telanito has the equipment that will connect us with all Nukutoans living abroad in our video conference. It is our opportunity to meet our loved ones, and together we can chart a way forward for us."

As the night wore on, the place was finally deserted as the islanders retreated to their homes for a good night's rest.

By 12 Telakitahuri opened his laptop to check if everyone was ready for their meeting. He had sent the link in the night and was hoping that everyone was online ready to begin.

He was surprised that everyone had been waiting for him, some for more than an hour. He was so eager to see those on the island, and there they were.

The camera focused on them and then to the screen. Just as he had anticipated, the screen was large enough for everyone to see. Relatives from all over the country and other parts of the world were all present for the meeting.

To begin their meeting, Telakitahuri briefed everyone on the purpose of the meeting. He then displayed the meeting's agendas for everyone to see. Before he opened the meeting, he allowed the chairman of the community government and other elders to make some remarks.

"Thank you, Telakitahuri for initiating this meeting and everyone who has attended or tuned in. This is the first of this kind and the first that we have come together as one people. Nukutapu may be have been destroyed, but not Nukutapuans as a race on the face of this earth. As long as these hearts pump in us, let us know that we, and our generations to come will carry this identity until fate determines otherwise. Although we may have relocated our home to Nukutoa, it doesn't mean we are safe from any disasters like the one that robbed us off our beautiful Nukutapu. Climate change will continue to have an impact on us. As we gather through this medium, I just have one message for all of us. Put our differences aside and work together for the good of our community. Never let greed, ego and self-proclamation come in between your people and you. I wish us all a fruitful discussion today," he said as the audience erupted into cheers.

After numerous speakers gave touching speeches, the meeting proper began and the agendas were brought into discussion. Everyone agreed with the formation of the Nukutoa Children's Foundation as a platform to drive efforts to protect the island from the effects of climate change and to safeguard the future of the children of Nukutoa.

Everything went smoothly as Telakitahuri had expected. He was elected unopposed to head NCF and everyone agreed to the vision that he had set for the island and its people.

"How did your meeting go?" Prudence asked when they met later in the afternoon.

"Everything went well as planned," he responded not too interested in continuing the conversation. It was the end of the week and he needed a break. "I feel that I need a break out of this place. How about us spending weekend with your family?"

"Or, how about watching a game of footy this weekend. The warriors and the PNG team are playing at Mt. Smart," she teased knowing how passionate Telakitahuri was about rugby league, and the PNG team as well.

"Are you serious?" he asked, looking into her eyes to see if she would chuckle.

"No, I'm not. Let's get our tickets and fly out to Auckland tomorrow. We'll watch the game on Sunday and return early Monday morning," she responded, and immediately began making online arrangements of their flights and their accommodation.

"I've never been to those big games. But I'm sure we'll enjoy," she confided after everything had been arranged.

The flight to Auckland departed at 3 in the afternoon. As Telakitahuri boarded the plane, he knew it would be one of the best moments he's had in New Zealand. The spectacular sight of Auckland city was breathtaking. He loved the place and could not thank his girlfriend enough for the opportunity to visit the city. Getting to stay in one of the best hotels in the city and then watching the game on Sunday made his weekend the most memorable one.

"So, how did you find your weekend in Paradise?" Prudence asked, as she sat on his lap after their return from the game.

"Wonderful! I'm enjoying every bit of it," he said as he planted a smacker on her lips. "Now I can return to complete what I've started.

When he returned to his room on Monday morning, the joy of having gone to watch his favourite team play was something he wished he could share with someone. He brushed aside the thought of calling Sione or his father when he realised he must get going to his classes.

After a month of hard work by Sione and all the other executives, NCF was eventually legally recognised. Plans of the various activities that the organisation intended to accomplish were all set out and ready for implementation.

"Look! The figures have gone up from when we last checked," said Prudence, showing Telakitahuri the latest figures of the Go-Fund-Me page they had created.

"Wow! A whooping $300,000! That's just what we need to kick start the activities of NCF," he exclaimed in delight.

"When we close that page, all the money will be transferred to the account that was created at Arawa. I'll check what programs they can start while waiting for my arrival. NCF is not a one-man organisation. I will have another video conference with the executives to see where we can start."

Juggling studies and his commitment to his community was challenging. But Prudence's charm made life seem like there wasn't a hassle at all.

"Soon we'll graduate from here. We've never spoken about this and I think this is the right time. What are your plans about us?" Prudence asked. She had been waiting for Telakitahuri to propose or say something about their relationship. But he continued to live each day like tomorrow was going to be the same. There were times she doubted his commitment to her but continued to push on with their relationship, thinking time will only tell when Telakitahuri will come true with his plans.

"To be frank, I love you dearly and don't see myself without you in the future. Why this all of a sudden?" he asked as he paused to look at her.

"I need you to make a decision now because I don't want to hang on to something that is not worth holding on to. You know what I mean. All that you are doing for your people means, you must return to your people," whispered Prudence, reduced by the complexity of her situation.

In her mind, was the confusion of whether what they had gone through all these years was real - or was it coming to an end? She had dreamt of building a family with Telakitahuri and now she was surrounded by uncertainty.

"My people and I came through the struggle of trying to make a better life for ourselves. Me being here in New Zealand doesn't mean I have to abandon my people for this good life here. I had a purpose in coming here and it is only appropriate that that purpose is fulfilled. As I've said numerous times, I love you. But you have to understand and bear with me as I sacrifice our time together to put perspective into the lives of my people. It will not be forever, and I plead for your understanding," he uttered with a heart that was full of love that need not be broken into two pieces.

It was a trying time for both Telakitahuri and Prudence: a test of where their love was heading. As their time at the university was coming to an end, a decision had to be made. The distance between New Zealand and Nukutoa was so great, that nourishing a long distance love can be tough. As time was drawing closer to their graduation and eventual separation, love and understanding between them seemed to have grown to another level.

"What about you coming over for Christmas?" asked Telakitahuri, as they met after class. Formal classes were coming to an end, with only the graduation ahead, and every moment together was precious.

"I'd love to! Are you ok with me coming over?" she exclaimed with caution as to whether it was all right with him.

"You know, I'd take you with me if you had no obligation to your family," he said sternly, and his face showed how serious he was.

"Really? I love you," she said, wrapping her arms tightly around him. "Let's just give ourselves time to sort our family and community issues before we commit to our plans.

The week leading to the graduation day had been strange, arousing suspicion in Telakitahuri about Prudence's behaviour. She spent more time at home rather than with him. Not being in the loop, Telakitahuri focused on his preparation.

Finally, it was graduation day.

With his mortarboard affixed to his head, and so handsome in his graduation gown, Telakitahuri sat amongst the graduands. Suddenly his mobile phone chimed - a text message from Prudence, who was seated a row behind him, to his left. He opened it and it read, "Stand up so that someone special could see you. He is in the crowd."

Telakitahuri stood up and looked. His eyes widened and his face grew pale with a sheen of sweat on his forehead at the sight of his father's face rising from the seated crowd.

Hadn't Prudence prompted him about that someone special, he could have fainted, thinking his father's spirit had appeared to him. In his culture, the appearance of the spirit of someone whom you knew was still alive meant he had passed on and was there to let you know he was gone.

He wanted to run over and hug his father but the graduation program was on and he could not do a thing. With tears rolling from his eyes, he blew him a kiss and sat down.

He knew it was Prudence and Teitione's collaboration to surprise him on his big day. The tears in his eyes didn't prevent him from sending a love emoji to Prudence and Teitione. And soon he got a message from Teitione that read "With Dad."

However, Prudence's message caught him off guard. It read, "You should thank your sponsor and your brother in-law. He was the one who organised the surprise."

It was a memorable day for Telakitahuri. He was surrounded by all those whom he loved, as he and Prudence celebrated their years of hard work.

"Cheers to Prudence and Telaki," screamed Prudence's father, trying to be heard above the noise of those who attended their graduation party. "All the best in your future endeavours."

It was a great party that Prudence's family threw for the two graduating lovebirds. In the presence of all those whom they loved dearly, they celebrated their hearts out.

It was the presence of his father that escalated the joy in Telakitahuri's heart. Although timid about the whole new experience in an environment that greatly differed, his father sat in his chair the entire night. He watched as his son and his girlfriend basked in the excitement of their achievements. From time to time he was engaged by Telakitahuri, Prudence and her parents in conversations that were barely audible in the midst of the loud music and singing.

"Father, now that you've come to meet Prudence and her family, what are your thoughts about my relationship with her?" asked Telakitahuri as he and his father exited the room for a private conversation.

"Son, I'm a typical Nukutoa man who would prefer that you married a girl from the island. You have your gardens and everything I own in the village to inherit. And I want the pure blood of Nukutoa to keep flowing for generations to come. However, what I want may not sit well with you and I understand that and won't stand in your way. You've built this relationship for years and I'm not going to undo what you have built. For the last four days, everything that I've seen and heard simply confirms that they are a good family. So, I'd say do what pleases you," said his father, sending thrills of excitement up Telakitahuri's nape.

"What? Four days! And where have you been staying all this time?" he asked but could not get an answer as Prudence swooped in to take the old man to the dance floor for a dance. Old as he was, his smooth slides across the floor took Telakitahuri by surprise as he watched from the side. The music was like it was composed for his slickness.

Three days after the celebration, Telakitahuri, his father and sister were on their way back to Arawa. In his seat, Telakitahuri put on his headphones, covered his eyes and lay back. Prudence's face was plastered in his mind as if it was undeletable. As the plane lifted off, tears streamed down beneath the eye mask.

Prudence had left her mark in his heart and that would take a long time to lose if their paths didn't cross again.

They arrived to a rousing welcome from their family at Arawa. Island dishes were lined up on the dining table in Teitione and Sione's house. His little nephews were all over him as he made his entry into the house. It was nice to see them again.

After greeting them and the others who were there, including his friend Telanito, he sat down for a bite as he chatted with Sione. The beaten taro in coconut cream and fried red emperor were tastier than he'd expected. And his munching and sucking of the juice that stuck to the bones of the fish kept interrupting Sione's explanation of what they've done in his absence.

Suddenly his phone rang. It was Prudence. He sprang to his feet with the intention of cleaning his hands before he could answer the call. To his horror, the phone fell from his grip and shattered its screen on the tiled floor. Picking it up, he tried to answer it but the shattered screen wouldn't recognise a touch. Sadly, the call rang out as he watched hopelessly.

Within the thirty minutes that Telakitahuri made his dash for the nearest mobile phone merchant, Prudence lay on her bed, daunted by his none response to her call. As she rose to find comfort in one of the spirit bottles that lined her dad's bar, her phone rang. She recognised that it was a Bougainvillean number, beginning with numbers that were similar to Teitione's number. Her heart beat as she brought the phone to her ear. It was indeed him, the guy whose voice she'd been longing to hear.

"Hello dear. I thought I was losing you after my call went unanswered," she uttered with a hope of some explanation of what had happened. She had felt awful after his flight out and the least she needed was to have a conversation with him.

Telakitahuri's explanation of what happened didn't matter to Prudence as she outlined her plans to join him at the earliest. Although he thought it was a great idea, he was concerned with what her parents would think. He knew her father had plans to introduce her to the company before operations wound down for the festive season.

But without wanting to upset her, he agreed to her plans.

After a week in the capital of Bougainville, Telakitahuri met with the executives of NCF. It was their first formal meeting where NCF's objectives and plans were laid out for everyone to see.

"If Dubai was able to build islands in the ocean, I see no reason why our God-made islands can't be made safer from the force of the sea so that we can continue to live on them," he began his maiden speech to the team.

"I know money moves things and that is the reason you and I have been appointed to lead this strategic team. So that we move things and make Nukutoa resilient in the eye of the Climate Change storm. Our reason for coming aboard must not be driven by greed, ego and political motives, but to give for the benefit of our community and generations to come."

The one-week meeting ended with the approval for implementation of key strategic moves that were necessary to drive the efforts of improving the lives of the people with short and long term goals.

Two key areas were the fortification of the island against the impacts of climate change and, second, the formation of the Nukutoa Children's Fund that will look after the welfare of the children, going into the future.

"These are key developments that need adequate funding. How do we expect to source these funds?" Teho asked, somewhat puzzled like many other members.

"When there is a will, there is a way," said Sione, fixing his trousers as he stood up to make his point. "We are a legitimate body that represents our people's aspiration for a better future. All we need to do is get our plight to donor agencies nationally and internationally to fund our programs."

Telakitahuri further supported Sione's views with a suggestion that caught the interest of the committee. They always thought the island had no potential for anything other than its human resources.

"Look at our lagoon. It is deep. It is huge, and would be perfect for tuna farming or any other type of marine farming. With the agreement of all our people, we can invite investors to come and invest in such a project. As a community obligation, they can assist with fixing our islands."

By the end of the week, it was decided that the first lot of help for the island would be on the next shipment in two weeks' time.

As the committee dispersed after their meeting, everyone felt relieved and glad that there was light at the end of the tunnel.

Preparations for NCF's assistance to its people went well, especially its Seawall Project. It was a collaboration with the member to provide basic materials for the construction of the seawalls. The Member for Atolls funded the gabion baskets and NCF procured cement and other materials needed. An engineer was also hired to oversee the construction works.

As the ship was finally ready to sail, Telakitahuri called Prudence to let her know he was on his way to the island. She was so happy for him and vowed to catch up with him in a few weeks' time when he was back in Arawa.

The next morning, MV Tausena poked its bow through avaiava passage. Standing on the port side watching the dolphins playfully gliding ahead of the ship, his eyes strayed to where his home once stood. The high tide seemed to have kept it under wraps.

Reminiscent memories of him and his mother sitting on that once lovely beach overwhelmed him with an incomprehensible feeling of sadness. Soon they came to the anchorage and the heavy anchor rattled on its way down. MV Tausena was locked into position and boats circled the ship ready to engage in the day's business.

On one of the boats was Lakia. He was ecstatic to see his cousin. His face brimmed with excitement as he signalled for something to drink. Telakitahuri reached into his cooler bag, pulled out a soda can and flung it out to him. He caught it with both hands, popped it open and drank it all.

"Refreshing! Long time," he exclaimed as he tossed the empty can into the boat. "Thanks bro. Welcome home."

"Thanks. There's lot to take ashore and we need our youth. Send word on any returning boat that we have building materials and other stuff to carry ashore," shouted back Telakitahuri.

After everything had been taken ashore, it was time for Telakitahuri to go to the beach. He climbed onto one of the boats. There was a strong stench of locally brewed coconut sap known as kareve all over the boat.

"Here bro, let's toast to the wonderful job that you are doing for our people," said Tekata as he offered him a glass of kareve.

"Just for the toast, I'll accept this glass and no more," he said as their glasses clinked together. "I have a responsibility to act decently as a man who has accepted the leadership of our organisation," he said and began to drink. It was perfect and although he wanted a few more glasses, but he did as he had said.

The boat arrived at the crowded beach. The passengers climbed out and made their way up the beach. As Telakitahuri walked, he heard Tekata telling his friends that he was probably interested in politics and may contest in the next election.

Chills ran up his spine. It was something that had never crossed his mind. Though he ignored the remark, he knew that his good intentions had been wrongly perceived. As he joined the others in sorting out the cargo, he felt troubled but continued as if nothing was wrong.

As the men started carrying the materials to the storage area, Telakitahuri picked up a coconut from the lot that were left on the sand, purposely for the new arrivals to quench their thirst. He cut the coconut open and was about to drink when he caught sight of some beautiful young girls watching him. He stopped to look. All the girls except Tukala had their eyes on him. She bowed, staring at her toes as she hugged her knees.

The troubles Tekata had caused him had all vanished in his mind as he instantly empathised with Tukala's state of being. He knew she must have heard about his involvement with Prudence and was upset about it. He wanted to approach the girls but then the Chairman of the Community Government called him over to discuss the launch of the seawall project to be held the next day. As he walked away, he promised to attend to Tukala as soon as he could.

After four weeks of working with the community to construct the seawalls that would minimise further destruction of Nukutoa, Telakitahuri felt a sense of satisfaction. The work was coming to near completion with only the eastern side to be completed. It was Monday morning and work was to begin early at 7 a.m. as high tide would come in at around 11 a.m.

The base of the cement walls to be erected needed to be strong when the high tide reached the spot of construction. Arriving on site an hour earlier with a few other men, they helped the project engineer to mark out where the structures would be built.

By 7, the engineer indicated it was time to commence with the construction. Telakitahuri looked around. There was something unusual about the day's work. More than half of the male population of the island was not present to help out as usual. He began to wonder if there was a problem back in the village that they did not hear when they left their homes. He thought about checking but then work started so he got himself immersed in the work and completely forgot about it.

The seawall began to take shape and the engineer's plan could be seen. The time to stop work was nearing and Telakitahuri left those completing the task and he walked away. Some metres away he stood and took a look at what they had done so far.

"Wow, great work!" he said to the men as other men also took steps back to appreciate what they've done.

At 11:00 as they predicted, the surging ripples of waves reached them, forcing them to retreat to dry land as the mothers assigned to cater arrived with dishes of creamed lobsters and local cakes known as hapopu. The day's lunch was Telakitahuri's request. As he ripped the lobster open, Prudence and her parents came into his mind. He missed their outings for dinner and the long chats that they used to have.

As soon as lunch was over, they proceeded with the construction of iron frames that were needed the next day. It was 5 in the afternoon when they retired to their homes, exhausted but glad of the progress they had made.

The next morning, when the same men turned up, Telakitahuri realised something was wrong. He excused himself from the working men and visited the community government office to make an enquiry. Equally puzzled as the other Community Government members, the Chairman immediately rang the bell for the villagers to gather.

Men and women, young and old gathered to hear what the Chairman had to say. For some of the men, they came prepared for a confrontation.

"It has come to my attention that many of you have stopped helping with our seawall project. Can we hear from you why this is happening when we are almost done with our project?" said the Chairman in his most clear voice.

Before the Chairman could go any further, Tekata stepped out. There was frustration in his eyes and those of the men who had gathered behind him. It seemed they had been waiting for this opportunity to express whatever grievance they had.

"We have ended our service to the project because we feel our community had been used by Telakitahuri to drive his political ambitions. He intends to stand in the coming election and is using our situation for that purpose," shouted Tekata, his eyes as red as fire as he spoke.

"We have Telaoi who came second in the last election to stand and wrestle this position from our current member. We don't need a young and inexperienced person like him to lead us."

Telakitahuri shook his head in disbelief. He couldn't understand how Tekata could have come up with such unfounded lies. He wanted to jump in and knock him out. But his lessons on Conflict Resolutions in Project Management had taught him well. He stood patiently absorbing all that nonsense.

As soon as Tekata's circus of drama ended, he calmly walked to the centre so that everyone could see him well.

"Thank you Tekata, for clarifying that your decision to influence all these men not to turn up for work, stemmed from your, and Telaoi's fear of my potential candidacy in the coming election. Am I correct?"

"You could just have approached me for clarification rather than distorting the minds of these men with your foolish and baseless claims. Regardless of my decision, our main focus should be safeguarding this island to prevent it from suffering the fate of Nukutapu."

"Frankly, individuals like you and Telaoi have been playing politics with the people's lives which contributed to Nukutapu's demise from the surface of this earth. I don't plan to run because if I'm not helping my community, I'd rather be in an office somewhere else," he said as calmly as possible.

Telakitahuri's sardonic response drew the ire in Tekata so that he responded aggressively to the young man. His desire for a physical confrontation was lowered by the raised voices of everyone around. As angry as he was, he put on a fake smile and calmly walked to the centre, where Telakitahuri had just vacated.

"You are such a show off," he said pointing his index finger at Telakitahuri. "Look at you. You promised to marry my cousin sister and now you've left her for a foreigner. People like you should not come and fool us," shouted Tekata at the top of his voice, drawing mixed reactions from everyone.

His intention to utter further insult was abruptly cut when the scrambling and grumbling stopped him from proceeding.

"Never involve me in your selfish and stupid intentions," shouted Tukala as she grabbed a handful of pebbles and threw them at her cousin. Her eyes told of her anger but not a line stretched to contort the beautiful face. Quickly her aunty jumped in to whisk her away.

Telakitahuri watched with a broken heart as Tukala cried as she was led away. The eyes around stared at both Telakitahuri and Tekata in bewilderment depending on whose side they were on as the whisper of gossip made its round.

Telakitahuri felt very awkward but he needed to man up to the situation. Eventually the chairman cut in to appease the situation. He asked Tekata to apologise to a deeply hurt Telakitahuri. However, Tekata took no heed of the Chairman's call. Refusing outright to apologise, he walked off, calling his supporters to follow.

Nonetheless, none of them followed, they felt Tekata had fooled them into believing all the lies that he had made up about Telakitahuri.

After things had settled, Telakitahuri shared his opinion, to which everyone concurred.

"If this is the attitude that we show those that have the heart to assist us find solutions to our problems, I believe our community will get nowhere. We must accept and embrace those who bring change to our community for the better. Yes, everyone has their shortfalls in life. But recognise the desire of those who bring with them their selfless passion to help our community and work with them. Let's not always dwell on the negative but the positive. What we have seen are impediments to progress in our society."

As soon as the meeting ended, Telakitahuri unashamedly marched to Tukala's house. He found her crying on her aunts' laps. Her hair strewn all over her face, wet by her tears of sorrow, self-pity and hatred for his cousin.

She looked up and saw him standing. She vented out no frustration, but deep in her heart there were questions that he alone can answer.

"Why did he allowed this to happen? Has he thought about what we've built over the years? Did he really love me? Didn't I show him enough love?"

The more she pondered over those questions, the more intense the feeling of confronting Telakitahuri became.

"Please leave me alone," she said calmly to him. Her swollen and red eyes told him how affected she had been. Heeding none of her words, he moved forward.

"Can I have a word with her?" he asked her aunt who without a word rose to her feet, tapped her on the shoulder and walked out of the house leaving them behind.

As soon as she was gone, Telakitahuri sat down next to Tukala. For a moment there was silence. The atmosphere was poisoned with an intense chemistry. He looked at her. Facing down, her hair hid her head and shoulders. There was an urge to touch her or to stroke her hair as he normally did but it was hard to lift his arm or even his finger.

They had agreed when he first arrived that they will remain good friends. But this was something else that was burning in him and he knew she felt it too. Then, she broke the silence in a shaky voice.

"Let's not deceive ourselves with these feelings. If it's not going to happen. Let's leave it that way." Her utterance gave him an understanding of the mutual feeling that still existed between them. He wished he could undo everything that had happened to him, but knew it wasn't worth wishing.

"I'm sorry," he managed to utter. "Didn't think my actions would lead us in this direction."

In soft sobs she whispered. "You didn't value what we have between us. It's been years that I have been thinking all was well; however, I now have to face the truth that there will never be an us. I am glad you found someone that you are happy to be with."

"I still love you Tukala. But I don't know if it's possible to have all the love I want in my life. Some days we have to make decisions that we have to live with. It might not be what we want but we must accept it," said a very distraught Telakitahuri.

Telakitahuri's words fazed Tukala. As much as she wanted to jump into his arms and beg to resuscitate their love, her dignity took precedence of any feelings she had.

"If it turns out to be not what we expected, I'll see you in the next life - if there is any. For now, I just need your last hug to be over all this."

It was a hug that neither of them knew how to leave. As Telakitahuri rose to his feet, Tukala looked into his teary eyes. She wiped her eyes as she whispered.

"You can be in another woman's arms but you will be always be in my heart."

Telakitahuri walked out of Tukala's house the most confused man in the world. He knew Tukala's love was genuine but he could not get to understand if there was a way, possible under the sun, to have both women in his life. Prudence too was exerting her claim over half of his heart putting him in a state of confusion.

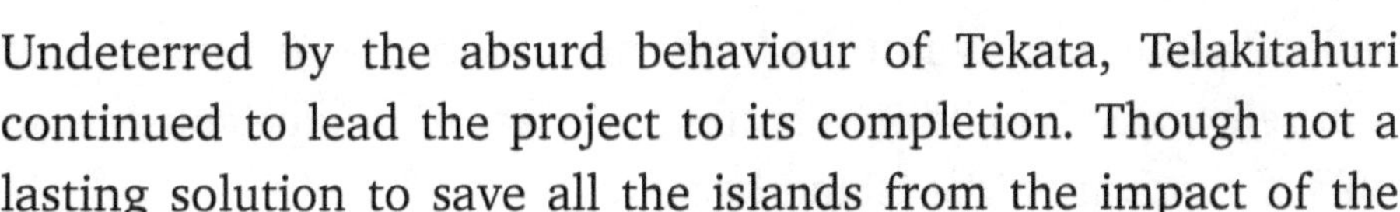

Undeterred by the absurd behaviour of Tekata, Telakitahuri continued to lead the project to its completion. Though not a lasting solution to save all the islands from the impact of the rising seas, it was a temporary measure to protect the wellbeing of the islanders till a lasting solution was found. The safety of his people superseded any other plans NCF had for the island, at least for now.

A day before Telakitahuri was to return to Arawa, a meeting was held to officially announce the completion of the seawall project, and for the Community Government and NCF to take onboard, the views of the people regarding several aspects of life on the island.

After key members of the community gave their speeches, it was thrown to the floor for anyone to express their opinions.

The first to come forward was Lakia. "I'm glad that we have risen up to take action to safeguard ourselves and our islands against the impacts of climate change. As we go each day, let us be reminded that these problems are not regressing but progressing. My question is, are we talking about resettlement as an option to our problem. I want to move out from here if there is land available," he ended his speech to the cheering and booing of the crowd. His words were supported by some while others didn't take it well.

Tepaia was one old man who listened to Lakia's speech with disgust. He believed relocation should never be a matter of discussion when talking about the future of Nukutoa.

"Lakia, this is personal. If you want to move out from here, go and buy yourself a piece of land and settle there. Do not encourage our people to move because that will never happen. We will not leave our island for somewhere else," the flimsy old man shouted.

He was the oldest man on the island and, the least he wanted was a relocation that will lead to the disintegration of the Nukutoa community into its host community. He further argued that relocation had its own issues and wanted it to be considered only if survival on the island became hard.

Lakia didn't accept the old man's words. He felt insulted by his direct approach about an avenue he believed discussions should be heading for the purpose of enlightenment on the issues affecting the community.

"Old man, you spoke as if you are able to paddle your canoe out to sea to catch fish, or to dig up the giant taros in your garden. Life is hard on this island and you must not sleep under the sweat of your carers and talk as if you are an able man," Lakia said angrily.

The Chairman interjected to keep the peace in the discussions and avoid people taking it personally or become frustrated by others' comments.

However, Tepaia wouldn't rest without coming up with comments that enlightened the people about his earlier speech. Though sarcastic, he wished well every ear that stood to hear it.

"My apology son, if this weak, old man has offended you. But I hope we all learn something in this meeting. Firstly, I would like to tell you that resettlement may be like entering paradise, yet, hell awaits you at the end of the day if you immerse yourself in the excitement and don't see that the devil was watching. I am old enough to know about all the resettlements that had taken place all over the world. And, today if you look at those resettlements, there is fighting between the settlers and their host communities, there is a loss of identity, the settlers' language vanished and many other issues are aroused. In this global community, the churches and the government called for love and unity amongst the people, but we read in the news about social and economic problems every day. Are you prepared to be resettled to another man's land and you and your generations to come to be socially and economically unsatisfied with life there?"

"Remember! You are a Polynesian minority in a Melanesian country. So, if you believe that a quick fix solution to your problem is what you want, resettle elsewhere. I was made to live amongst the fish, and this is where I will stay and demand that my government spend money on me here rather than take me to a place I will not be happy to live," said the old man with tears rolling down his wrinkled eyes.

There was a lot of ideas shared. Some relevant for consideration while others not worth the ear at all. Telakitahuri offered no word as he wanted to listen to everything that the people had to say.

Finally, the day to return to Arawa arrived. The islanders as usual, were preparing food especially for those departing to take with them.

After packing everything that he was offered, from fish, clamshells and many other choices, he left his house for a walk about. He wished he could give Tukala a last goodbye before he left the island.

Passing Tukala's house, his eyes secretly pried into and around the house. She was nowhere to be seen. However, he was caught off guard when Tukala, watching him from a house nearby emerged to surprise him.

"Were you looking for me?" asked Tukala with the brightest smile that she could put on.

"No. Not at all. I was just passing by," he said with a smile in return. "What made you think I was looking for you?"

"Well, why would a man like you be passing my house and looking around as if he was looking for something. I thought we were done," said Tukala as she held his hand and led him into the house.

"It's complicated to answer all your questions, but I guess I wouldn't want to leave today without seeing you," admitted Telakitahuri.

"So you getting on the ship today," she quipped.

"Yes I am," he responded with a smile.

"Take this laplap," she said as she extended her hand to him. There, in her hand, was a nice floral laplap.

Their hands came together and instead of taking the laplap, he pulled her closer to him. He wrapped his hands around her and kissed her forehead. When he released her, there were tears in her eyes. With his fingers he wiped them and stared into those eyes.

"What's wrong?" he asked, hurt by the tears in her eyes. He hated being put into a position he must make up his mind. He was not prepared to forego Prudence nor Tukala.

"I must tell you that Telanito's father knotted my hand for Telanito few days ago. This will be the last time we share anything between us. I hope you accept it and understand my situation. I need to have a man, just as you have a woman," Tukala's voice trembled with pain.

It was a practice on the island that when parents liked a girl for their son, they would tie a knot on the girl's hand in the presence of her parents. And that was what Telanito's father did. He didn't know about Telakitahuri's relationship with Tukala and knew Tukala was the right one for his son.

Tukala's revelation of Telanito's father's act wounded Telakitahuri. And he wasn't leaving with the hope that the laplap would be his source of strength for the time being. He needed to express himself and, the more he stood in front of her, the pressure within built up.

"How could you have accepted Telanito's father's proposal? You know how close Telanito and I are. Is it your way of getting back at me?" he calmly uttered, masking the storm brewing in him. He was not ready to accept Tukala in another man's arms, even his best friend Telanito, and yet his manly dignity forbade him from openly displaying that hurt in his heart. "This is an injustice!"

As the clock ticked to MV Tausena's departure time, Telakitahuri sat on the seawall waiting for the canoe to take him to the ship. His admiration of the men's fine work on the seawall brought poetic lines into his mind as he watched the surging tides rolled up and down the beach. Soon they would caress or pound on the seawall in whatever might they came.

*You think you'll break me?*

*I'm harder than you think.*

*Made to withstand what comes your way.*

*Though I love your gentle rubs and coolness,*

*I'm hard for your cruelty.*

*And I will protect my purpose of being.*

By 3 in the afternoon, Telakitahuri climbed onto his cabin bed as the engine of MV Tausena rumbled to life, beginning their voyage to Arawa.

There was too much in his mind to watch the vast ocean stretched out into the horizon. The coolness of the room was right for a well-deserved rest. He closed his eyes and went to sleep. In the wee hours before morning, MV Tausena reached the mobile network coverage. The chiming of his phone from messages flowing in woke him up.

While on the island, he never bothered to hook up on the Wi-Fi as he was always busy with the project.

He looked at the messages. Many of them were from Prudence. The last one, which had been sent about a week ago read, "Still waiting for your call." He wanted to call, but then hesitated. The rumbling and revving of the engine wouldn't allow a good conversation.

Instead, he started uploading photos he had taken on the island onto his Facebook account. He watched as his friends reacted and commented on his post.

"No sign of Prudence," he whispered to himself as he lay on his bed. "She must be mad at my non-response to her messages. If she decides to leave me, that's fine. I'll concentrate on what I'm doing."

As the ship came to berth, Telakitahuri looked out of the porthole. Several islanders were on the wharf, waiting for their relatives who were on the ship. Some were waiting to receive something from the island, such as dried fish, dried clamshells, sweet island coconuts and many more.

He looked beyond the wharf expecting to see Sione's car. There was no sign of the car or anyone he was interested to meet on the wharf.

The passengers began disembarking. He didn't move. He remained on the bed looking out through the porthole. The wharf began to be crowded. Just then he thought about the call he was supposed to make to Prudence. Quickly he got onto his feet, collected his stuff and headed for the gangway. His hands were full and he needed to return. As he descended onto the wharf, he heard a familiar voice call his name. He looked down and there was Prudence, surrounded by his nephews.

Surprised, he nearly dropped the stuff in his hands. He was happy to see them and they too were equally glad to see him.

After hugging the kids, Prudence melted into his arms. The smell of her favourite body fragrance and the warmth of her body reminded him of how much he missed her.

"When did you make it here?" Telakitahuri cried, pushing her head some inches away so that he could look her in the eyes. "Almost two weeks now," responded Prudence with coyness as the curious islanders stared as though someone had miraculously risen from death.

It was terrible with the many eyes on them. After introducing Prudence to some of them and bidding them farewell, they hit the road to Toniva.

"Now that you are here, I'd like to visit Buin and Buka. Sione and Teitione have taken me all around here and, I tell you, it's such a magnificent place. Lovely people and beautiful vegetation. I love it here!" she joyfully said to Telakitahuri.

"I'm happy you love the place. Have you been to the mine area? It's an attraction that most visitors to Arawa never wanted to miss. The bloody war that took us backwards 20 years was all due to that mine. It has its significance in the short history of this young nation," he responded boastfully.

"Yeah, we were there. Every ascent to those mountains, fills you with awe, revealing beauty that transcends mere scenery. It's a reminder that nature holds secrets more magnificent than the view itself," she uttered with an honest insight into what she saw on her visit to the mining area.

"The visit to Buka and Buin will happen after I have a meeting with the executive of NCL," he said and the conversation ended.

Prudence sat quietly. She was disappointed. She wanted Telakitahuri to leave whatever he had in mind and spend time with her. The silence was deafening when Sione broke it.

He suggested that Telakitahuri take a one week break from all NCF-related work and spend some time with Prudence. Shrugging, he agreed with him and promised to start with the Buin trip.

Prudence woke up to find Telakitahuri busy with his tablet. Spread out on the table was a map of Bougainville. It had all tourist attraction sites marked out clearly. Beside each site were descriptions of the significance of the sites.

"I've planned our trip to Buin. We'll at least spend three days at Buin, drive around the Siwai, Panguna road and to Buka. We'll spend a week in Buka before returning to Arawa," he explained, hoping that she would be interested.

"Whatever!" responded Prudence, showing no interest after he had brushed aside her suggestion for the trip the previous day.

Knowing that she was still upset, he went ahead packing items that were needed for the trip. Finally the car he hired online was delivered to their doorstep. Without much said, Prudence climbed into the car. Telakitahuri started the engine and off they drove to Buin.

It was around 10 a.m. when they called into Louai Township for a little refreshment. Standing beside the vehicle, they discussed whether to go into the cafeteria or to go into the market. The bananas, pineapples, mangoes and many other local produce were too enticing to miss so they headed into the market, picked up what they wanted and left the area.

A kilometre from the Louai market, an old man was in sight.

"Could he be from your island?" asked Prudence, pointing to the man whose complexion and features resembled Telakitahuri. Beside him were two bags of cocoa destined for the market. As they made it closer, Prudence could see that the resemblance to

Telakitahuri couldn't be mistaken. The obvious too had dawned on Telakitahuri, however he wasn't in for a wild guess.

"Let's check him out. I have a long-lost uncle whom I've never seen. My father told me he is married to this part of Bougainville, but I'm not sure which village," said Telakitahuri as he pulled the vehicle up next to him.

Alarmed by the stopping of the vehicle beside him, the man put down what he was holding and stared at Telakitahuri who poked his head out of the rolled down window.

"Good day. Are you from the Atolls?" asked Telakitahuri as he stared into the man's eyes as he too stared back into his eyes.

"Yes, I am," responded the man as he moved closer to Telakitahuri not taking his eyes off him.

"You must be my uncle Polos!" cried out Telakitahuri as he opened the door and jumped to hug his uncle.

Prudence watched as the men embraced and expressed the joy of meeting each other for the first time in their lives.

"Small world here but, how could their paths have never crossed for this long?" she wondered.

"My village is down this road. I could take you there for a look but I'm on my way to Buin to sell these bags so, perhaps any other time you come by, call in," said Polos to the approval of his nephew.

"Let's give him a ride to Buin since we are on our way there," said Prudence to Telakitahuri.

"Good idea," replied Telakitahuri.

As the two men were putting the two bags of cocoa into the boot of the vehicle, Telakitahuri whispered into Prudence ear and she quickly collected her stuff and jumped into the back seat. Surprised that he was taking the front seat, Polos looked into his nephew's eyes and smiled.

"Your father had raised you well. And you," he said as he turned to Prudence. "I'm impressed by my son's choice of a woman," he added as he extended his hand.

"Thank you. Nice to meet you," responded Prudence.

The ride wasn't long when they started to ascend the Leulo Mountain. At the top, Telakitahuri parked the vehicle. Prudence followed him out and they stood enjoying the breath-taking view in front of them. Drifting to the south of the tip of Buin were numerous islands that were part of the Solomon Islands.

"I didn't think the two countries were this close," said Prudence as she took a selfie of the two with the spectacular view in the background.

"We'll see if we have time to run across and back. Get in and we'll move. We've got to reach Buin by midday," he responded. Soon they were on their way down the slope onto the Tabago Plains. It was a slow drive with all windows open and the cool breeze blowing into their faces.

Suddenly a large billboard appeared in front of them. They came to a stop metres away to take a look.

"Do you think we should check it out?" asked Telakitahuri not really sure if it would be a great site to visit. The billboard advertised the spectacular Murugiruno Resort that had a panoramic view over Buin as far as the nearby islands of the Solomons.

"This is definitely a must-visit resort in our next trip up this way," said Telakitahuri. "Look, there is a tramway to take us up and down. We can also go kayaking on Lake Lulolu."

"Why not?" responded Prudence. "Drive in."

"Now that we know about this spectacular holiday resort, we'll definitely come in the future. Too, uncle is on his way to Buin so we can't delay his time," he said as he continued their drive to Buin.

Dropping off the old man, they pulled up at Failen's Café where they ordered lunch and headed straight to the Yamamoto Crash Site.

"What's the significance of this site," asked Prudence as the Tour Guide led them to the area. The place was nicely looked after. A variety of flowers decorated the path leading to the crash site.

"Admiral Yamamoto was a brave Japanese airman during World War Two. The shooting down of his plane by the Allied Forces was one of the events that led to Japan's defeat in the war," explained the guide as Prudence nodded in agreement.

She had no knowledge of such events in the past as she never took history very seriously.

After their tour of the site, they headed straight to one of the best resorts in the area, the Mangira Beach Resort located at the Kangu Beach. Telakitahuri had first heard of the place from some relatives who once spent their holiday there. Beautiful bungalows lined the white sandy beach. And not too distant, was the breath-taking view of the islands of the Solomons.

Having their dinner of coconut creamed lobsters, Telakitahuri's eyes could no longer stay open. Leaving Prudence to continue her dinner alone, he put on the air conditioning and climbed into the king-size bed.

In no time, the splashing of the waves on the beach faded as he drifted into dreamland.

The bright morning sun streamed a lot of sunlight through the silky satin curtains.

Opening his eyes he reached for his tablet. He slept early and wanted to check if he had any messages or missed calls. There was an email that had come in last night. He quickly sat up, opened it and read, "We are pleased to notify you that we have considered your proposal and we are impressed. Our staff will reach out to you to communicate our final decision."

He jumped out of bed overly excited about the news.

"Hey, what's up!" cried out Prudence, shaken by his abrupt movement out of bed.

"I've got to share this great news with the committee," he responded as he proceeded to get dressed.

"What news?" she asked, staring at him not knowing whether to be mad over being disturbed in her sleep or wanting to hear what the good news was.

"I received an email from the International Donor that we requested assistance from," Telakitahuri answered.

"Wow! That's great!" Prudence exclaimed as she sat up, "But you ought not to cut short our stay here as I'd love to spend some more time here. Give them a call instead," she insisted.

"No, I have to tell them in person," he informed her apologetically, with a look that begged for no resistance.

"Fine. Take a ride to Arawa instead. When I'm done here, I'll drive back," she retorted in the hope that her message was heard.

Telakitahuri knew he wasn't getting it his way. The last thing he wanted was leaving his woman there all by herself.

"Let me see the email," Prudence demanded, extending her hand for the tablet. He passed her the tablet and she frowned as she read the email. Shaking her head, she said to him. "You are being so skittish. The final decision is yet to be made. So don't give them false hope. Wait till you receive the confirmation and then you can share the good news with them."

"You know what, I think you are right. Get back to bed while I get some breakfast," he said as he opened the door.

"Don't want anything I've tasted before. My coffee and something local," she shouted after him.

After some time, Telakitahuri led the waiter in. He set out a small table on the bed and turning to Prudence he said, "Fried wild fowl eggs, baked breadfruit biscuits and hot cocoa made from locally brewed cocoa beans."

"Wow! Fantastic! I know I'll love it," she said smilingly to the man who shyly returned her smile as he excused from the scene.

Prudence sat up straight and smiled at Telakitahuri as she began to spread the egg over the biscuit. She took a sip of her drink and then had a bite of her food.

"Wow! This is good," she said to Telakitahuri, with a mouth closed so that she didn't spew out her mouth's content.

In a few minutes, the table was bare, with only the dirty cutlery and Prudence craving for more.

"I'll request that for lunch too if that's possible," she said to the waiter who had returned to clean up.

"Our organised tour around those islands is leaving in an hour. Would you two be interested to go?" enquired the waiter.

Before Telakitahuri could say something, Prudence shouted, "Wonderful! We'll be at the jetty soon."

The day's tour was awesome. Their ferry toured the coastline of Buin before turning to the islands of the Solomons. On two islands they went ashore and spent time at their resorts.

Finally, it was time to return and the Solbrews were beginning to have an impact on the visitors. It was a fun-filled day and, by 6 in the evening, the couple was too tired and hit the sack straight away.

The revving engine of a boat arriving at the resort's jetty woke Telakitahuri up. He looked at Prudence and she was snoring her nose off. Peering through the window glass he saw three fishermen on the boat. They were Solomon Islanders of Kiribati origins from the nearby Kamaleai Island.

Quickly he rose to his feet, locked the door behind him and walked to them.

"Any rainbow runner amongst your catch? I'd love to have one," asked Telakitahuri, looking into the men's boat as his hand rested in his back pocket ready to pull out his wallet. He noticed several cut-up fish next to dry coconut shells and knew he had come to the right people for his favourite dish.

"You want to have it raw?" asked one of the men as he rose to his feet, handing Telakitahuri a rainbow runner, a dry coconut and a knife.

"How much is this breakfast you are giving me?" he asked with a smile that looked like a tooth exhibition.

"It's our pleasure to offer one of our kind our island delicacy," said the one who offered the fish. "Get on."

Telakitahuri climbed into the boat, sat down and dipped the fish into the sea as he cleaned it. He cut up the fish and then began to eat it with the coconut. After finishing his meal, he thanked the men and returned to his room.

"Wake up, Prudence. We have to hit the road for Buka," said Telakitahuri as he shook her by the arm.

"What time is it?" Prudence asked, yawning and stretching her arms and legs on the bed.

"7," he responded and proceeded to the shower. "Man. Yesterday's tour just wore me flat out," she conceded as she turned on the bed. She wished Telakitahuri wouldn't rush them on their way as she needed more rest.

After taking his bath, Telakitahuri playfully ushered Prudence to the bathroom. He needed to speed up their travel as there was a lot in his mind regarding the activities of NCF.

The drive through Siwai, Nagovis and Panguna was enjoyable, especially for Prudence who loved to buy fruits and vegetables from the roadside markets just to have a chat.

At around 11:30, they stopped at the Morgan Junction to have something for lunch and then continued their drive to Buka. They arrived in time, just as the ferry was loading to cross the Buka Passage.

"Look, that guy looks like he's from your place," Prudence said pointing out someone paddling a kayak against the fast-flowing tide towards Sohano.

"I wouldn't know if he's from my place or from the other two islands - Nuguria or Nukumanu. Yes, Buka was where most of our people settled because it is our regional town. Also, many of my people settled here during the post-crisis era. The lack of shipping services to the islands at that time forced many families to leave the island in search of better schools for their children, to be closer to health services and, perhaps, to make ends meet as there were absolutely no economic opportunities back on the islands at that time. Maybe everything stemmed from the poor leadership of that time and the fact that the Buka people were such good people who freed up their lands to accommodate not only our people but everyone else who was looking for a place to stay," Telakitahuri continued.

Booking into the Kuri Resort, they sipped a few glasses of wine before retiring early for a good rest. At 10 in the night Telakitahuri's phone rang. Prudence heard the melodious ringtone and woke him up. He sat up, picked up the phone and answered.

"Congratulation!" came a man's voice on the other side. "Your organisation has been considered as one of the recipients of our assistance to Climate Change impacted communities all over the world. An email has been forwarded to you. Take note of everything that was stated in the email so that we can progress this project without delay. My name is Shaun and I am the man assigned by my organisation to deal with your project."

Telakitahuri was lost for words. All he could say was thank you, thank you and the call ended with them agreeing to speak again so arrangements can be made for their travel into Bougainville.

He turned to Prudence, hugged her and then got out of bed and started pacing here and there in their room.

"Settle down!" exclaimed Prudence. "Get a good rest and tomorrow we'll see how things go."

"Yes. I think I will get to meet all the islanders here and break the news to them. But firstly, I will have to call Sione and the committee in the morning," he said as he slipped back into bed.

News reached all Nukutoans in Buka that there was going to be a meeting at Sohano, and they came in numbers. Telakitahuri arrived alone as Prudence went sightseeing.

He was met at the jetty by an old man by the name of Teone, whom, as he was told, had inherited the role as Nukutoa Sohano Community leader from his uncle. He found him to be a man of humour and commanded a lot of respect from the community.

The place was full of people, young and old. They all gathered to hear what the news was. After formal introductions, Telakitahuri began to tell them about NCF and its functions. Everyone seemed uninterested in what he spoke about. He knew they expected more than just a few words to them.

He then decided to give them time to speak. He wanted to know what they had in mind.

A small elderly man walked to the middle. "I am very grateful that you have come up with a great initiative to help restore our island. My only question is, do you have any programs to help people like us who have no means of making ends meet here. We have settled here and established families. But life is hard here. Many of us are unemployed and, with no land for gardening, life is challenging," he said with sadness in his eyes. He ended his speech to the loud applause of those in attendance.

"NCF does not take the place of our leaders in finding solutions to our problems. Its main concern is to rebuild our island so that those of us who can't make a life here, can return home and live a village life – a life that is not pressured by land lease payments and the extravagant town lifestyle. Only after we achieve our objective, then we will start looking at ways to improve the socio-economy on the island as well as create a fund that will take care of the future education of our children," he responded and the response didn't seem exciting to them.

He understood their situation and knew it was a task NCF had to address as soon as possible. Telakitahuri was still thinking about what to say next when a young man approached hastily. He moved to the side to allow him to speak.

"In the past, such organisations were established only to disappear without a trace of what happened to funds that they'd accumulated through fundraisings and donations. What guarantee can you give us that this isn't one of them. I issue this warning that this time, we will allow no one to walk free. We will either man-handle you and your executive or make you answerable to the law," uttered a young man, as Teone moved closer and whispered into Telakitahuri's ear that the young man was affected by substance abuse and needn't be taken seriously.

Nodding to Teone, he stood up. There was something about the young man that caught him, and that was his desire to fight for what his people truly deserved.

"I envy your courage young man. We, young and vibrant youths in our community must have a positive impact on our community. Yes, some may have misled us in the past. But I do know that there were others who had tried their best but failed due to many circumstances. It is our duty to pursue our people's struggle against these hardships. Let's not sit and expect the climate to change for the better, for the sea to stop battering our islands, for economic growth to come by and our children's future be handed to them on a golden plate. We need to rise up together with hearts that are full of passion, determination, selflessness and not be driven by greed and ego," he said as everyone roared with applause.

"Let me inform you all that, in the near future, an international funder will arrive in Arawa and transit to Nukutoa. On Nukutoa, we will sign documents that will allow us to rebuild our islands - not only to fortify them against the cruelty of the sea, but to make sure you and I are not part of the statistics of people who have nowhere to call home."

As Telakitahuri and Prudence drove back to Arawa, he felt satisfied and accomplished, even though the real work was yet to begin.

A week back from Buka, the words of the young man kept echoing in his mind. He was adamant those were the sentiments shared by every silent Nukutoans whose desire for change kept being denied by greed and personal interest.

He knew those self-oriented values would follow suit if he and his executives didn't have the people at heart. In their meeting, he stressed his expectations to all the members and was glad the people's choice of the executives was a perfect selection.

Preparations for the arrival of the team from overseas had been flowing smoothly under the supervision of Teho who was tasked to organise it.

A dance troupe from the island was given the privilege to welcome the visitors at the airport. Even on Nukutoa Teho's instructions for them to prepare for the team's arrival on the island had been well received. Traditional dance practices could be seen all over the island. There was a celebratory mood building up there.

Booked to make her return to New Zealand on the day of the team's arrival, Prudence quickly called the airline to rearrange her travel upon learning of all the celebrations that had been planned. It was an opportunity she didn't want to miss.

"I've rebooked my return for next week. It's an opportunity for me to see your culture in display," she said to Telakitahuri after receiving the response from the airline.

"Perfect! I don't want to be caught in between worrying about you and playing my role in the meeting with the donors," he confessed from his heart, making Prudence think hard about whether she should return, take him with her or stay for good in Bougainville.

"I'm prepared to do anything for us to be together forever," she said. "And how about persuading my dad to make an investment here. I see lots of opportunities. I could head here to manage the business."

"It depends on whether you meet the criteria to invest in the Bougainville economy," he jokingly said to her.

"And what criteria would that be?" she asked, frowning at him.

"You have to be married to a Bougainvillean," he responded as he burst out into laughter.

"You've got to be kidding me. Of course, I am. I'm getting on that chopper to get my customary blessings that I am officially your wife. Like that woman in one of your photos with all those turtle ornaments hanging on her neck and arms. I'll demand that!" she joked as she too burst out laughing.

Though she sounded as if she was joking, her heart cursed him for playing with her situation. She would beat any legal system just to make sure she was beside him for the rest of her life.

The executive met again to finalise the program which was then circulated to all Nukutoans. Many expressed their desire to witness the grand signing on the island.

Unfortunately, it was too short a time to arrange with MV Tausena's Management for a trip to the island. Although many were not pleased with the decision, they had to accept it as the ship had other commitments to fulfill.

"Wow, I'd love to be on the island to see the display of culture on that grand signing day," said Prudence as she looked at the program. She had heard numerous times of how things happened on the island. She always wished she had the opportunity to see that and experience it firsthand rather than hearing it from Telakitahuri. It will be a historic moment for the islanders. There were big events held on Nukutapu but not the newly settled Nukutoa.

The islanders sprang into preparatory mode with dance practices everywhere on the island after they got the news. The men and boys practiced several dances such as the rue, takere, knife dance while the ladies practiced the toha, hula and ladies' rue. The release of the program gave the islanders some clues as to what will happen that day; however, information regarding what the visitors would offer, remained a secret - with only the executives in the loop.

A day before the arrival of the visitors, the executive arranged five speed boats to travel to Nukutoa: two to take essentials that would be needed on the day of the visitor's arrival and the other three to take the executives and few others who wanted to join the celebrations on the island.

Surprisingly, Prudence and her father in law's names were on the list of people to travel. Her insistence was a thing Telakitahuri couldn't handle. So he asked his father to accompany her.

With whatever they could take, they drove to Kieta so that they could get on the boat. They arrived to find the boats loaded and just waiting for the last two passengers to board before they could depart.

Prudence and her father in-law got on and just as they were about to leave, the unexpected happened.

"Stop right there!" came the order from a lone Disaster Prevention Officer. "You are overloaded and some of you need to get off." Everyone on board looked at the latest to get on. Sadly, it was Prudence and her father in-law.

They reluctantly got off and watched as the boat sped off.

"Don't worry, we'll find our way," she said to the old man. "Telakitahuri, find us something comfortable to travel in."

Quickly Telakitahuri did an online search for any boat available for immediate hire.

"What about this?" he said, showing her a picture of a boat that was available.

"No. Find something big and comfortable," she responded. "That one isn't big enough to my liking."

It was not long before Telakitahuri found a boat he believed was perfect for the trip. He excitedly showed Prudence the photo and she liked it.

"Wow! Seahorse is just perfect. We'll take it," exclaimed Prudence.

Overly excited by their find, she proceeded to make the call to the owner who sent details for the transaction to be made and the boat was good to go. However, they had to delay to give Telanito, Teitione and her children time to prepare. They too were now keen to go. Finally, the four-day hired speed boat which was owned by an expatriate miner was soon on its maximum speed to the island.

With the perfect weather experience, the 200-mile journey would be a smooth four-hour adventure. As the boat made its turn around Pokpok Island, Telakitahuri and Sione got into the car and drove back to Toniva in silence.

The vast seas holds its dangers, but it was the confidence that the boat would reach the island that kept them strong. They were looking forward to an early bed time, however their light dinner of bread and canned tuna was disturbed by the arrival of several cars outside their home. It was the troupe of island dancers who needed some guidance in how they would welcome the arriving team at the airport the next day.

With Teho gone already to the island, they needed some guidance from Telakitahuri and Sione. As the rehearsal was on, Sione's phone rang. It was Teitione, who had called to let them know that they had arrived safely. He whispered the news to Telakitahuri and walked away to chat with her.

Telakitahuri continued watching the rehearsal, however, expectantly hoping Prudence would call to tell him how she was doing on the island. He was worried about her. As the dancers packed into the vehicles to return to their homes, Telakitahuri picked up his phone and dialled Prudence's number. The call went dead. He tried Telanito's number - with the same result.

He looked at the time and realised it was late, and by then, the Wi-Fi on the island was already off. Getting into bed wasn't an option as his mind was still on Prudence. He poured himself a glass of his favourite wine, picked up the guitar and settled on the sandy beach. He played the guitar and sang some hulas as he sipped his glass of wine.

The sound of waves splashing on the beach and the sight of crabs playfully crawling on the sand with their shiny eyes glittering in the reflection of the moon, reminded him of home. He wondered if Prudence liked the reality that she had arrived to. As he made his way back into the house, past midnight, he assured himself that all was well with her.

Telakitahuri woke up the next morning to the excitement of the day's event. As the arrival time drew nearer, a convoy of cars hit the road to Aropa International Airport.

At exactly 10 am Bougainville Standard Time, Bougair taxied on the runway to a halt in front of the terminal. The four men in suits were led to the waiting dancing troupe of youths who swung their knives viciously around their bodies as the circling girls swayed their arms and hips.

The visitors were caught off guard and were amused by the performance put on for them. They took pictures and then moved on to meet the committee, who were accompanied by the Member for Atolls. Young girls adorned woven leaves on them and then they moved on to shake hands with some of those who were there to meet them.

"On behalf of our Nukutoa community and our MP, we welcome you all to this beautiful nation of Bougainville. We hope that your short stay will be a memorable one," uttered Telakitahuri to their guests. After one more performance by the troupe, the entourage departed for Bovotel to freshen up before their next activity.

Half an hour later, they arrived at the chopper's landing pad a passenger more than the flight could take. The MP had begged to be included bringing the number to seven.

"Hello gentlemen, unfortunately we can only carry six passengers at a time," the pilot regrettably informed them as he pulled his tightly fitted overall garment that looked as though it was chiselled to his ebony body so that he could climb into his seat.

The MP, knowing he would be the one cut off from the trip, stepped forward to have a word with him as the others climbed into the helicopter. The pilot called Telakitahuri out.

"Since we have no cargo, I can allow him to get on. However, with only six seats available, I would suggest that you, being slim and fit, sit at the back.

"No problem at all Captain," responded Telakitahuri as he and the MP climbed in. The chopper roared into motion as it lifted into the air, and darted straight for the Mortlock Atoll. The pilot announced that the flight would take approximately 45 minutes.

In the excitement of the moment, the passengers stared out at the wonderful landscape that they left behind and the ocean that stretched out as far as the eye could see.

After 30 minutes, the atoll was visible. Telakitahuri removed his Canon camera from the bag and passed it to Sione, who was seated next to the pilot to take the shots. Soon they were over the western 80 part of the lagoon, heading straight for Nukutoa. Those with cameras swung into action, taking photographs of the islands below. They flew over Nukutoa, then turned south and approached Taku and over all the islands till they reached Nukutapu - which was now just a dune of sand. It hovered above the sand and then slowly it touched down on the sand.

Everyone got off and walked around the sand dune, making their assessments and discussing important aspects relating to the project.

Behind the sun-shades that covered his eyes, tears rolled down Telakitahuri's face as they stood right at the spot where their house once stood. Memories of his late mother in their happiest moments in their house flashed in his mind.

"Looking at the islands on our way here, I noticed that the largest island isn't inhabited. You can all move to that island and not be bothered by the rising seas," interrupted Shawn's voice.

His eye sparkled in delight as if he had found the answer they never knew. Telakitahuri and Sione glanced at each other and then fighting off the sadness that had overwhelmed him, Telakitahuri spoke.

"Taku is the name of that island. You know, that island functions like the heart of the atoll. Once it is inhabited, food stocks may not be as it used to be, increasing the prospect of starvation on the isolated atoll," Telakitahuri responded.

"We can find ways to mitigate the challenges of climate change, but once we destroy the purpose of that island, that would be the end of life on this atoll." Shawn was amazed at the logic behind Telakitahuri's explanation - 200 miles to Kieta and 350 miles to Nukumanu, was a great deal of a distance to travel to bring food rations should food shortage be experienced.

Finally, it was time to move. The chopper lifted into the air and flew to Nukutoa. Looking down as the chopper glided in waiting to ascertain its landing spot, everyone could see celebratory fever building up below. As the chopper came down, the trees seemed to mimic the dancers below, swaying to the beat of muscular men on their wooden drums.

Nukutoa was alive with celebrations. The place was all yellow with the islanders in their traditional attires surrounding the landing pad to welcome the VIPs, defying the threats from the force of the rotor on their laplaps.

One by one, the VIPs climbed down. They were amazed and honoured by the display of gratitude shown to them. They were then led to the Marae, where the five clan chiefs, elders and members of the community government were waiting for them.

Shaking their hands and welcoming them to the island, the Chairman of Nukutoa Community Government then ushered them to their seats.

He then introduced the five clan chiefs as they shook hands with them on the people's behalf. As Telakitahuri took his seat, he looked at the audience and his heart almost melted in his chest.

His beautiful Prudence was all draped in yellow, indistinguishable among the islanders. Her white complexion was covered in yellow with turmeric powder, yellow woven aralia leaves on her head, decorative turmeric leaves around her neck and fastened around her waist was a mehau woven out of tree fibers.

His attention on her was interrupted by the Teariki's chant for the opening of the Marae to the program and to welcome the VIPs to the Marae. The Master of Ceremonies then officially took over as he led the program by inviting the men's rue to perform.

The visitors chatted to each other as they watched in amusement, fascinated by the movement of the dancers in sync to the sound of bamboos beaten with sticks. After the dance ended, various speakers of the community were called to make their speeches. Finally, the moment they had been waiting for arrived.

"Good day everyone. My name is Shaun. On behalf of my visiting team and our organisation, I would like to thank you all for the warm welcome and hospitality accorded to us in Arawa and here. My organisation assists communities impacted by climate change by funding programs aimed at reducing these impacts. Going through the Nukutoa Children's Foundation's proposal for funding of its activities, we were surprised that your community had been through so much. You have been trying your best to mitigate these problems all by yourselves, with no outside assistance. Your gardens were affected by salinisation. Your islands were being eroded at an alarming rate, and the saddest part was that Nukutapu was being reduced to a mere sand dune as the world watched. We sympathise with your struggles. No community on this earth deserves to face such hardships. Your resilience has inspired all of us," said Shaun, the leader of the visiting team.

He then picked up a coconut that had been placed on the table in front of him and took a sip. "Marvelous!" he exclaimed and proceeded with his speech.

"Today, I am pleased to announce my organisation's donation of these funds to fund activities identified by NCF," he said as the people erupted into cheering, dancing, and for some like Telakitahuri, tears of joy flowed freely.

After Shaun's speech ended, Telakitahuri, as Chairman of NCF, took the stage to convey the people's gratitude to Shaun, his team and their organisation.

He then directed everyone's attention to a huge banner that was being unveiled as Sione pulled down the curtain that covered it. It was an artist's impression of what the Mortlock group of islands would look like after the completion of the project. There was jubilation all around as a deafening applause rang out. As shown, the works will include connecting Taku, Nukutoa, Nukuahare and Karuteke together with a splendid beach front with the northern, eastern and southern sides protected by seawalls that were further protected by mangroves.

"Listen carefully. These funds will guarantee us that we will have a place we will call home for another fifty years or so. Only our maker can foresee what will transpire after that. Whether he gives us another opportunity like this to fortify our island against the impact of climate change or relocate us to safer grounds," Telakitahuri screamed for everyone to hear.

Numerous heart-felt speeches were made and then dances were performed to entertain the visitors. As the dances continued, tables of a variety of island dishes were set out and the visitors were invited to serve themselves. They ate as they watched the display of the island's culture.

Telakitahuri asked Prudence to join him. They served their meals and joined the others on the stage. Prudence was amazed by everything.

"What's your opinion of the day's event?" Telakitahuri asked.

"Wow! I'm speechless," she responded as she took a bite of a hatuke, meat of sea urchin that had pencil-like spikes wrapped in a pandanus leaf. "You not only have an unblemished culture, not overly affected by modernisation, your food too, especially seafood, is amazing."

The celebrations went right into the night. By 10 pm, the village youths took the four visitors and the pilot to a house specifically made to accommodate them. They had to get some rest before their return flight the next day.

Seeing that their guests had gone to bed, Teariki rose to close the Marae. People began moving to their houses. As Telakitahuri looked at the bright moon, he recalled how, when Taku was a little boy on Nukutapu, he would come out and watch the young taupus and taupearas hula to the tune of ukuleles and guitars.

"Teariki, would you permit us to hula tonight," Telakitahuri asked the retiring Teariki, who was a cheerful man who liked to give the young the freedom to entertain themselves in traditional ways, as long as they behaved themselves.

"Go ahead grandson," he responded as he toddled with his cane to his utta - a special space that only the Teariki can sleep on. The taupus and taupearas quickly gathered their guitars and ukuleles and the hula began.

Telakitahuri sat with his guitar and beside him was Prudence, relishing the excitement of everything that was going on. Soon the instruments came into play and singing of the hulas followed.

"How sorrowful. The effects of climate change. So heart breaking...." The dancers in synchronised steps, began going around them, swaying from side to side as they went.

After five hulas, Telanito took the guitar from Telakitahuri. "Take your girl for a dance," he said to him. Telakitahuri was reluctant, but seeing Tukala behind Telanito, ready to take Prudence's position, forced him up. Without a word, he pulled Prudence up and they joined the long line of dancers. Prudence found it hard, but she tried anyway.

As they danced, Telakitahuri could not cope with the sight of Tukala beside Telanito. He felt insulted by his own friend and the girl he loved. But he knew it was right anyway. He wasn't going to commit to her and knew his friend would look after her just like he would have.

The dancing continued till daylight broke. Shaun and his men heard the singing and joined them as the pilot made his way to prepare the aircraft for their return to Aropa.

"Would you want to have a glass of this?" Lakia asked Shaun and his men. "What is that?" responded one of Shaun's men as he took the glass.

"It is called kareve," responded Lakia as the man smelled the content and shook his head in disgust.

"Take a sip, it is good, just the smell that will bother you," said Lakia, trying to convince the men to take it.

The man took a sip as his eyes squinted at the bitterness and smell of the beer. In his life he hadn't come across such as this.

"Wow! If only that awful smell can be eliminated. I'm sure there is a way. I promise I will return with a way you can improve this beer and commercialise it if you agree," he said to the approval of Lakia as he began pouring glasses for each of the men.

Finally, it was time to take the departing team to the chopper for their trip back to Aropa. The walk took a long time as the men, loquacious under the spell of Lakia's concoction, took every opportunity to engage with whomever was near them.

Eventually they were packed up and the aircraft launched into the air and away it went, minus Telakitahuri. He had decided to give Prudence some precious moments on the island before her return to Arawa and, eventually, back to New Zealand. After seeing off the chopper, Telakitahuri gathered the youths before his planned departure later in the day. He had brought two dart boards and arrows and a table tennis set - things that they had requested when he last visited.

"I wish to present these items to you, the youths of Nukutoa. This is the beginning of better things to come for you all. NCL has plans to turn you into skilful artisans in the near future. We will run training programs here meant to equip you with skills that you can use to earn a living," he said, as all the youths attentively listened.

The presentation was fast as Telakitahuri planned to take Prudence sightseeing around the islands.

As they were dispersing, an unprovoked Tekata, who was passing by, directed some offensive and derogative abuse at Telakitahuri. This caught them off guard.

Telakitahuri quickly moved to calm the enraged youths who were about to jump on Tekata. They watched as he raised his right hand up forming his fingers into a pistol shape. With a swift motion, he fired into his head, conveying a threat to Telakitahuri. The youths were determined to take him down. But Telakitahuri's words calmed them.

"These are the actions of desperate men who see good men as a threat to their evil intentions. Let him be. At least I know that I need to be cautious with every move I make," he uttered with a voice shaken by a restrained frustration.

"We are all behind you and will continue to support you to bring the best for our people," said Tekosi, the youth leader who continued to lobby for the youth's and community's support in the efforts of NCL to bring change to the island.

Just before midday, Telakitahuri took Prudence sightseeing around the many islands that made up the Mortlock atoll before turning the bow of the boat to Kieta's direction. The sea was like clear glass that spread out as far as the eye could see. It was a glide that Telakitahuri's nephews loved. Their squinting eyes stared at the sea ahead with the full force of the wind as the two 200-horsepower engines gave it all its might.

With large headphones over his ears, the best of Tavake Band amplified in Telakitahuri's ears like there wasn't an engine revving and rumbling at his side as he watched the islands gradually growing small in the wake of the high-powered engines.

As he watched the furthest islands disappearing, he thought about his father. And felt great sorrow for him. He had refused to return with them, opting for his simple life on the island.

They were thirty miles out of avaiava Passage when Prudence tapped him on the back. He turned and Prudence told him the skipper had something to say to him. Balancing himself, he approached the skipper who had the steering device in one hand and his binoculars in the other. His staring into the apparatus alarmed Telakitahuri who begged to know what he was looking at.

"Take a look," he said as he passed him the binoculars. Telakitahuri drew the binoculars to his eyes and looked. Instantly, Tekata's act earlier in the day flashed through his mind. Although the boat was drifting half a mile and ninety degrees to port, with no sign of life on it, his instincts told him there was danger.

The skipper asked if they should have a look in case the boat was in a state-of-emergency situation. Remaining calm, and not wanting to alarm everyone on the boat, he ordered the skipper to alter course ninety degrees to starboard and increase speed.

The skipper did as asked and after five minutes of watching the boat through the binoculars, Telakitahuri began to see heads rising from the inside of the boat.

"Pirates!" he screamed to the shock of everyone on board. Teitione began to cry as she held tight onto her kids. Prudence's face went purple with fear. There was intense fear in everyone's eyes as they all looked at the pursuing boat, hoping that it won't catch up.

"Don't panic," said the skipper to everyone. "We have an engine that can outrun them by miles. "Calm down." Pulling out a satellite phone, he asked Telakitahuri to handle the steering device as he dialled his boss' number. Immediately his boss picked up the call.

"We've been pursued by pirates and need police assistance," shouted the skipper into his satellite phone.

"Oh my gosh! Ok, Ok. I'm calling the police right away," responded the panic-stricken owner.

Immediately the police were notified of the situation. After minutes of mobilising their manpower for the task at hand, they got in touch with the skipper. Details of the boat's location and the speed they were cruising in were all taken to map out their rescue operation and shortly after their call was disengaged, the Bluebird and Bluemarlin were dispatched.

The skipper returned to the helm of the boat and Telakitahuri picked up the binoculars. He got to the back of the boat, crouched next to the engines and drew the binoculars to his eyes. He scanned the sea and there was the boat, still pursuing them. He felt safe with the distance between them, but was hoping the police would show up soon. Any mechanical issues would be disastrous for them. He watched them carefully.

There were four men in the boat: the skipper and three men all with high-powered guns in their hands. Their heads were covered in balaclavas. One of the men with guns was taking an aim at them.

"Get down!" he screamed and everyone ducked for safety. The shots were not heard. But he knew, they either missed or could not reach them. "Accelerate!" he shouted to the skipper. "They are firing at us!"

"Don't worry. At this distance their shots can't reach us. We are keeping them in sight for the police to arrive," responded the skipper calmly.

After 20 minutes of pursuit, there was still no sign of the bluebird in the air. Agitated, Telakitahuri kept watching their pursuers and scanning the sky for any sign of the bluebird with the binoculars.

Suddenly the skipper tapped him on the backside and passed him the satellite phone. There was a message, which read: "Slow down, we can see you."

As the skipper pulled the throttles down, Telakitahuri quickly drew the binoculars to his eyes and turned to the pursuing boat.

After five minutes, one of the men stood up to see why their boat had slowed down. Suddenly, he pointed to the sky and the boat made an abrupt turn south towards the Solomon Islands border. They knew border restrictions would limit the chopper's pursuit if they could reach it.

But the pilot was smart. Instead of making a bee-chase, he flew towards the border, turned and glided in waiting.

The men fired at Bluebird as they made a U-turn. Seeing a policeman take his aim, the pirates quickly jumped into the ocean as their boat's engine took several shots and with a huge explosion, engulfed in fire, shooting flames high into the sky. Helpless as they were, the four men could be seen swimming away from the inferno.

Bluebird approached the swimming pirates. As it hovered a distance away, a policeman screamed through a hailer for the men to raise both hands up. Seeing that they were no longer a threat, they threw lifejackets to them and disappeared, rerouting to Nukutoa.

Half an hour later, Blue-marlin arrived at the scene. The policemen pulled the men onto the boat. From a distance, Telakitahuri, through the binoculars, watched the policemen beating the pirates after pulling them onboard, putting handcuffs on their wrists.

The Seahorse's radio cracked and rumbled to indicate a radio message was to be received. Then, a voice came through. "Seahorse, Blue-marlin calling, over."

"Go ahead Blue-marlin, over."

"What is the name of the guy Bluebird is to pick up on Nukutoa? Over."

"Tekata over. Tango, Echo, Kilo, Alpha, Tango, Alpha, over. Out."

"Roger, Roger. Head straight to Kieta beach. Cheese"

As Blue-marlin came to berth at the Kieta wharf, Seahorse's bow touched the sandy beach of Kieta. Although safe from the ordeal, those on board were terribly shaken by the experience. However, the many eyes that stared from the shore made the moment awkward to handle for the distraught passengers.

News reporters who wanted to have a story for their media organisations sought them for their story. Telakitahuri stepped forward to tell their story. Suddenly the cameras turned to the pirates as they were ushered to the waiting police vehicles to be taken to the station for interrogation.

As the attention shifted to the pirates, Telakitahuri, Prudence, Teitione and her children got into the car and drove to Toniva. They were relieved to be out of the extra stress the journalists had put them through.

"You've got to pack your bags, because I'm not leaving you behind." Prudence said sternly to Telakitahuri on their way to Toniva. Everyone was silent. It was an experience that could have cost them their lives had the Bougainville police not been equipped to fight such crimes and their boat not fast enough to evade their pursuers.

"Look, this is an isolated incident that involved desperate and greedy people," he finally responded, "We Bougainvilleans, are some of the best people you can find on this earth, although we had twenty years of bloody war. When the time is right, I will join you or you can return for me here," begged Telakitahuri for her understanding and peace at mind.

They arrived to a house full of relatives and friends who have heard the news and had come to wish them well and bring them food. Tears were shed as they welcomed the family from their near fatal return trip.

After sometime, Telakitahuri received a call. It was from the police station. They wanted his statement of the incident. He took Sione's car and rushed to the station and gave his statement. After an hour, he returned back to the house.

It was late in the afternoon, when everyone left for their homes, that they settled down for a well-deserved rest. Dawn came creeping into their abode indicating it was time to begin another day.

Teitione was the first up. After a quick spray of water to her flowers, she got into her husband's car and drove off to the nearby shop to get breakfast. Twenty minutes later she returned to find everyone waiting for a warm breakfast. As she and Prudence got themselves busy in the kitchen, Sione dragged a chair closer to the table and dropped into it as he spread the paper over the table.

"What a shame!" he exclaimed, as his finger followed each word as he read. "Instead of your name and picture appearing on the ballot paper in six months' time, it is now on today's newspaper. And it's because you let Tekata's greed cloud your wisdom."

Telakitahuri came behind Sione and looked at what he was talking about. There on the front page, was a photo of Telaoi, Tekata and those whom they had hired to eliminate him. There was no grudge in his heart, but sympathy for Telaoi's children, who will be without all the love that a father can offer. He shook his head as he returned to his seat.

"You have the potential to be a leader and that was why they feared you. Would you be interested in raising your hand in six months," asked Sione as he bloomed with keenness in what Telakitahuri's response would be.

"That's a no, no, no," shouted Prudence from the kitchen to the support of Teitione. "I don't have to be a Member of Parliament to be able to do good for my people. Yes, the position comes with power, influence and money to move things. But if the heart is not with the people, that power, influence and money can go to waste, with the people not seeing a dime of their money," he uttered with satisfaction in his heart, demonstrated to Sione through his cordial smile. It was clear he had the heart for his people, but politics, at that moment was not his desired medium to make things happen. Time was a healer.

As the days went by, Prudence's stance of taking Telakitahuri with her back to New Zealand softened, and he was able to convince her to let him lead NCF's projects on the island.

Eventually the day came for her to return to New Zealand. They arrived to a packed Aropa International Airport. Prudence joined the queue to check-in while Telakitahuri stood watching the queue moving at a snail pace. He was lost in his thoughts, when he suddenly felt an embrace from his left side. His senses returned and he looked down to see Prudence head just below his chin. His eyes quickly went back to the queue and he realised that in his thoughts he hadn't realised Prudence had checked-in. He quickly wrapped his hands around her and led her to the side, away from the path of those trying to check-in.

The embrace seemed different. There was an intense longing for each other that neither of them wanted to leave. Emotions took the better of them as the boarding announcement echoed through the terminal. In her tracks, out of Telakitahuri's embrace, she stopped, turned back to him and uttered. "I've got to get checked up when I get home," she managed to say in between sobs. Her make-up completely ruined by the rolling tears and constant wiping of her palm.

"Why!" alarmed he uttered - with the utterance almost choking him".

"I think I'm pregnant," she responded, and felt terribly sorry for Telakitahuri as he wept with joy.

"I'll see you soon. First, I've got to make sure that my child will have the opportunity in future, to see where Papa called home," he shouted to the departing Prudence.

Watching Prudence take her stride to the ladder of the plane was difficult. The dark sun shades over his eyes were flooded with the effect of his broken heart, and he wished she would turn back and cancel her return one more time. He felt like he wasn't ready to let her go. When she reached the door of the plane, she turned and looked back.

There was a desperation for him in sight, but the tinted glass walls of the terminal were unkind to her moment of despair. She waved, hoping that he returned it from wherever he was as she disappeared into the plane. Telakitahuri knew he had to be strong. Most of the time he was the one who left a broken Prudence behind in New Zealand and now it was his turn.

Now it was not Prudence alone that he thought about. The little him in her had connected him to her like never before and he was miserable.

Prudence alike was devastated. She loved her man dearly, but things had to be like that for now.

As the plane climbed into the sky, Telakitahuri's gaze followed till it was only Prudence that he could visualise. He climbed into Sione's car and the playfulness of his nephews eased the sorrow that had engulfed his heart. He assured himself, determined like never before to begin NCF's plans for Nukutoa as soon as possible. And it better be fast, in case Prudence needed his support.

Two months after Prudence's departure, there was no sign that NCF was ready to begin its major project on the island. The biggest obstacles were the systemic slack whilst clearing the funds. The prolonged delay resulted in unfounded rumours being circulated around the Nukutoa Arawa and Kieta communities that the funds had been mismanaged by Telakitahuri and his executives which was the reason why none of their projects had materialised.

"What's the latest on NCF's land reclamation project?" Tekata asked a group of boys who visited him in prison after more than twenty minutes of sharing the gospel with him. The iron bars had kept him from freedom and even hearing the slightest news about his community's happenings.

"Nothing has been said about it lately. The last we heard was that the funds had arrived but needed to be cleared by our banks," responded one of them. "You know what? Telakitahuri may have diverted the funds to his wife in New Zealand. I know how the educated conduct their affairs. They invest such funds in stocks and when they make enough money, they return the funds. If the investment failed, we lose everything and then they blame the banks for not releasing the funds," went Tekata with his predictions of what the cause of the delay could be.

He twisted the minds of the boys to think Telakitahuri had been up to no good with the funds. And he played his game well. When the boys returned from their visit, Telakitahuri was on every Nukutoans' lips. Those that came to visit him, hoping to be included in the project's implementation took their distance. The matter was even reported to the police who took Telakitahuri and Sione into the police station for questioning.

"What's the reason for this invitation?" asked Sione, shaken by the unexpected invitation by the cops.

"There has been a complaint laid by some Nukutoa elders that the two of you, including the other executives of NCL, had spent funds intended for the land reclamation project on the island on unrelated expenses. Can you clear the air on that?" asked the policeman who was there to question them on the issue.

"We are not going to explain to you, unless we know who the complainants are. Can you bring them to the station so that we can explain to them in your presence?" said Telakitahuri. Two policemen got in the vehicle and drove away.

Telakitahuri and Sione waited in the room with the other officers. After the policemen had been gone, Telakitahuri told the officers that they were yet to access the funds as there had been some issues that the bank needed to clear up. After half an hour, the policemen returned without anyone accompanying them.

"The complainants don't want to show up. They want us to question you about those funds and inform them about our findings," said one of the policemen.

The officers who had been waiting with Telakitahuri and Sione weren't happy. One of them got in the vehicle and asked the policemen to take him to the complainants. After less than ten minutes, they returned. With them was the Chairman of the Nukutoa Community Government and two of his members.

Telakitahuri and Sione could not believe that they were the ones who lodged the complaint. They have been briefing them about the reasons for the delay and they don't know what made them think they were not honest with their explanations.

"Now that you are here, you can now proceed with your complaint," said one of the officers, urging the Chairman to speak.

"We received some rumours that NCI's executives, especially Telakitahuri, had siphoned project funds to his girlfriend in New Zealand to trade in the stocks and that was why we were alarmed and decided to involve the police. We were mandated by our people to safeguard their interest and we believe what we did was in their best interest," said the Chairman with some caution.

As the Chairman spoke, Telakitahuri shook his head in disgust. He didn't know where those lies had come from. He wanted to shout abuse at the Chairman but he had a lot of respect for him.

Then the police officer asked him to respond to what the Chairman said.

"Chairman, I have a lot of respect for you. But I'm dumbfounded by how a man of your calibre could believe lies and would not have the courage to approach me directly for an honest explanation. Just a week ago, I informed you all about the difficulties we had in accessing the funds. Our people's affairs shouldn't be dealt with on the streets. There are proper avenues that we can handle them. Tell me where you got your story from. That is a clear case of character assassination," said a distraught Telakitahuri.

The matter was settled with everyone happy that the funds were never mismanaged.

"The heart of a Nukutoan must always prevail over any disagreement we have with each other. That was what our parents taught us to be on the island," said Sione as they vaisonied and hugged each other on their way out of the police station.

Telakitahuri's investigation led to Tekata as the source of the lies. He heard Tekata and his band of criminals were to be in court that day so he paid him a visit at the waiting cells.

"You will never break my spirit. You will rot with Satan in hell. Our community is lucky to be free from demons like you, who have nothing good to offer but their evil influence," said Telakitahuri to a smiling Tekata.

"Enjoy the peace behind those walls. They will make you a better person."

Then, the unexpected happened. A few days later, news arrived from Nukutoa that the eastern seawalls that had been constructed recently had been battered by high tides, shattering the cement walls to pieces.

The news irked Telakitahuri and Sione, who protested outside the President's office for his intervention to clear up the funds so that works on the island could begin.

As promised, the funds were cleared. A meeting was convened by the NCL executives with those contracted to do the job. The scope of work to be done were clearly outlined for all to know.

As mobilisation was taking place, Telakitahuri and the contractor's management travelled to the island by chopper to make the islanders aware of the works that would be done. Community awareness on the project had been carried out earlier and the current awareness was only for the islanders to absorb the scale and magnitude of the works to be done and advise them not to put themselves in harm's way when machinery of all kinds arrived on the island.

When the party returned to Arawa, Telakitahuri remained on the island. He would be there for the entire construction stage of the project.

Finally, the first shipment arrived. The contractors sunk two long poles that stood 20 metres up from the surface of the sea close to the reef. A signboard was put to show the people the specifics of the project as well as portray the outcome of the project through an artist's impression.

"Impressive!" cried Teariki to the agreement of Telakitahuri and those around as the entire population on the island stood on the beach watching the workmen's amazing work. Everyone cheered with admiration at the wonderful display of Taku, Nukutoa, Nukuahare and Karuteke all connected to create one big island.

"Telakitahuri, I forgot to raise this issue with you. You see the point of Taku facing Nukutoa?" asked Teariki as he pulled Telakitahuri to the side. "I see that on the signboard all those areas will be covered and a wharf to be built at the middle of the two islands. Can you appeal to the contractor to spare that area just close to the shore of Taku known as Teavava Kahaniti? That is a sacred area of our ancestors. In the past one of our clans used that area as their burial site. I am sorry if this is late but do your best," said a worried looking Teariki.

Teariki was optimistic that developments of such was needed on the island, however, he was steadfast that sacred areas must remain undisturbed to honour the culture that sprouted since the beginning of time on the island.

Today's generations owe it to the past generations, whose choices, experiences and expressions had shaped this unique identity that distinguished the people as Nukutoans. He believed that now that the island has embraced changes such as infrastructural development and the introduction of social institutions that try to shape the society's values and behaviours, those changes must be seen to have a positive impact.

"Thank you Bubu Teariki," said Telakitahuri. "I admire your wisdom and definitely I will ask the contractor to alter its scope of work to cater for your request. That is how projects flow. We work together with those who are here to help us to create the best for us."

In the days and weeks that followed, the beach of Nukutoa came alive with ships, machinery and people arriving to commence work. The plans were now implemented to connect Taku, Nukutoa, Nukuahare and Karuteke together.

The first task was to block off the channel of water that ran between Nukutoa and Taku. Large blocks of bricks were lined up along the eastern reef from Nukutoa to Taku to slow the incoming waves from where the sea normally broke.

Telakitahuri sat on the reef watching the men at work. The reef was dry and he thought about several times he and his friends caught fish by running after them as they swam to reach the deep.

Suddenly his phone rang. "What! The Wi-Fi signal can reach here!" he exclaimed as he reached into his pocket. With a click of his finger, Prudence's face appeared for a video chat.

"How are you dear?" came Prudence's voice as she stared into Telakitahuri's face on the screen. "Your face looks black in that hot sun. Put on some sun screen."

"We are made to be like this. Don't you worry," responded Telakitahuri taking off his sun glasses and hat for her to see how the sun had impacted his skin.

Telakitahuri and Prudence's conversation lasted an hour as they talked about many things. She also confirmed her pregnancy to a very elated Telakitahuri who announced to all those around that he was going to be a father.

After their conversation he headed home to tell his father about the news. He was only on site to see the progress of the work and had no role on site as he was only there on behalf of NCL to monitor the progress of the work. On his way home, he met Telanito who just returned from his fishing trip.

"Hi taina, come around my place for dinner. I looked all over the place for you so that we can have raw fish but you weren't around so I asked my wife to prepare it for dinner," said Telanito who was going to change after bathing in the sea.

"Thanks taina, I'll see you at 6 sharp. I've got to share some good news with my father," called out Telakitahuri as he continued on his way.

"Anything that I should know too, taina?" shouted Telanito after him.

"Oh okay," he said as he turned and walked back to Telanito. "Prudence is pregnant and I'm over the moon," he shouted as he raised his hand to hi-five Telanito.

"I'm so happy for you taina. Congratulations!" responded Telanito. "Well then, meet me at 6 sharp so that we can toast with a cup of fish soup to that."

After sharing the news with his father, who was also very happy for his son, he took a short nap and woke up in time for his dinner with Telanito.

After several months, the project's progress turned up just as planned. The workers admired their work but the islanders were over the moon as they watch everything unfolding in front of their eyes. Taku had been connected to Nukutoa, Nukutoa had been connected to Nukuahare, and now work was in progress to connect Nukuahare and Karuteke.

The turnout was magnificent. The beach fronts were reclaimed a hundred metres into the sea and, sea barricades were constructed to attract the build-up of sand along the beach. The island was paradise in the making.

To the southern end of Taku, the youths planted mangroves on the reef towards the passages. It was all done to slow down the sea currents that enter and exit the sea lagoon and to create a habitat for a variety of birds and fish. It will turn the area into a wildlife reserve, larger than the current one.

Every night, Prudence would video call and the two would spend an hour or so chatting with each other.

"Do you think you can make it here before I go into labour?" Prudence asked one night, as she focused the camera over her heavily pregnant belly. She wished he was around for the baby shower.

"As much as I'd like to, I can't make it on time," he regrettably said to her. "The ship just returned to Kieta four days ago. Its next voyage to the island will be in three weeks' time. By then, you could have gone into labour already."

There was sadness in Prudence's eyes and, he didn't like it. He jumped up from his bed, picked up his torch and made his way to the beach. Under a solar light that lit up the sandy beach that had been reclaimed some meters into the sea, he knelt down on one knee and proposed to Prudence to marry him right where he was kneeling.

"Yes! Yes! Yes!" Prudence cried, overwhelmed with joy. She didn't think about what her parents would say about the venue of the marriage. The distance and the cost of getting there never came into mind as she started conversing with Telakitahuri on what they wanted for their wedding.

The next day she shared the story with her parents who were caught off guard by her decision to agree to a wedding far away from home and all her relatives and friends.

"Please discuss with Telaki if it's okay to bring the wedding here. You know how much I don't like being away from the business," begged her father. "We can assist with the cost of getting his family here since I insist on having the wedding here."

"Dad, it's not about money or whatever, that we want our wedding to happen there. Look at this," said Prudence as she showed her father all the work that has been ongoing on the island. "This is what Telakitahuri has been doing for his people. His people are so at peace with their life on the island; however, the sea was about to make them refugees against their will. To honour his struggles for his people, I agreed to have the wedding there. I wouldn't mind if you and mum, relatives or my friends don't make it to my wedding. It is a life that I chose to have and I am having it the way I wanted it. No matter the distance, no matter the strange environment, no matter the kind of people, my baby and I will be there for the wedding."

Prudence's choice of words touched her parents' hearts. The last thing they wanted was their only daughter sad. They both approached her, hugged her and promised to support whatever decision she made.

Back on the island Telakitahuri sat his father down for a father-son talk. This was important in his life and he wished his mother was around for the discussion.

"Father, I proposed to my girlfriend to marry me here," he said.

"What! You are bringing those high-class foreigners to this island! You know what their paradise is like, yet you decided to bring them to this hell of a place? No. I don't want us to be humiliated when they arrive to find this tiny island isn't what they wanted for a wedding venue. I beg you find another place to have it," said his father, totally against his idea to have the wedding on the island.

Telakitahuri was shattered. He became withdrawn, visited the project site less, hardly talked to anyone and the saddest part was his phone was off. For months, Prudence has been trying to get in touch to no avail. Stressed by that, she called Teitione at Toniva to check if she had the opportunity to talk to him lately.

"It's been a while since he last called us. Sione too had been alarmed by Telakitahuri's lack of feedback on the progress of the project. I will try calling him or father," said Teitione.

After failing to connect to Telakitahuri for many days, Teitione called her father. "Don't know what happened to him," said the old man. "He stopped talking to me and I hardly saw him visit the project site."

"When did that start?" asked Teitione surprised at what has happened to her beloved brother.

"A month or two ago, I think. He told me he planned to have his wedding here. I told him that I would be ashamed if Prudence's family, turned up to find this place not the place they want for their daughter's wedding," recalled the old man. "Am I wrong to have said that?"

"Off course you did not have to tell him that. He's a man now and can reason out what's best for him. You are the cause of his condition. And, where do you expect an unemployed man like your son to find the money to have his wedding in the kind of place you have in mind? He thought bringing the wedding to the island will incur him no cost as a village wedding does not cost much money,"

Teitione said calmly, wishing her words gave her father a lesson to learn. And indeed, he took it hard upon himself. A week later Sione arrived on the island to check on the progress of the project since Telakitahuri failed for many months to update him. He was sorry to see how withdrawn Telakitahuri was and so he made the effort to talk to him and bring him out to help with the preparations for the completion of the project.

"Whatever problem you have, you need to come out and help me organise the ceremony," said Sione to Telakitahuri. "Please I need your assistance. Shawn, his team and government officials will be here and I want us to put up an event that really shows our appreciation."

Although Telakitahuri agreed to Sione's request, the hurt deep in his heart could be noticed. He had no will, no commitment and no motivation to do as Sione asked. Instead of him taking the lead, Sione was the one now taking the lead.

In spite of Telakitahuri's issue, NCF was ready with its preparation for the closing ceremony. That morning of the ceremony Sione and Telakitahuri stood at the newly developed beach front of Nukutoa that extended all the way to Sauma at Taku and to Karuteke.

Neatly attired to meet their guests who were to arrive by chopper at 10, they sat under the large make shift tent erected for the ceremony when a commotion was heard coming from the village. Quickly they went to investigate.

"What happened?" Sione asked a young man who was running past them. "There's a fight there. Two women were extending their boundaries over the newly reclaimed land and they could not agree on their borders. Their quarrels were intensified when their husbands joined in with a fist fight," explained the young man.

"And where are you running to?" asked Telakitahuri confused by the young man running away from the scene of the fight.

"My uncle Hipatu is one of the men and I am going to tell my other uncles to come and help," said the young man.

"Son, stop right there," called Sione. "There is no need for you to do that. Follow us and we will go and solve the problem."

A crisis management meeting was immediately called and all the islanders were summoned to attend. They all attentively sat to listen as the Community Government Chairman expressed his disgust at the intention of a few who were laying claims to land reclaimed under the project.

"We are still to show our appreciation to those who had made the land reclamation project a reality and a success and already some of you are fighting over these lands. Please have some decency and stop these greedy acts. As of today none of you will lay claim to any land on this island accept the portions that you currently occupy," he shouted as everyone listened quietly.

"As agreed between my office, the Council of Chiefs and NCL we were going to spell out the terms of portioning all this land that is now available to our people after today's ceremony. But since we are now all here as a result of this morning's fight, I will ask NCL's executives to present what we have agreed in our meeting."

Sione and Telakitahuri revealed the portioning of the reclaimed land to the amazement of the islanders. Some of them had been dreaming about putting up modern homes but customary taboos on the types of houses that could be built and, the lack of available spaces in the village had shelved their dreams.

As Sione spelt out the process of distributing land through a body made up of representatives from the five clans and various sectors of the community, the roar of the chopper's engine could be heard. Minutes later, everyone sprung to their feet and made their way to the place the ceremony was to be held.

As they fell into their positions, the chopper made its landing, and out came Shaun and his delegation. There to receive them were community leaders, NCF executives and Bougainville Government dignitaries who had arrived by speed boat some minutes earlier and had been at the venue while the islanders were in a crisis management meeting.

"Looking south, north and east, I can see why there are smiles everywhere. And thankfully, I understand that smile. If my organisation wasn't made aware of your island's dire situation, you all could be part of our statistics of refugees in the near future. I am happy that your fear of the island being further eroded and that you will be homeless in the near future, has been resolved or addressed by the completion of this project," shouted Shaun into the loud hailer.

After the ceremony was concluded and Shaun's team in the air on their way out of the island, the sound of an engine roared from the lagoon. Everyone moved around altering the setting of the arena.

And Telakitahuri, he stared in confusion. What was happening next was not part of NCF's program. "What is happening now?" he wondered as he tried to give a hand where needed.

"A sea plane!" exclaimed a little boy as his mother pulled him away. Confusion clouded Telakitahuri's mind as he watched the place being transformed into something like a church.

Then, the pastor appeared in his ceremonial robe at the altar. As the tuneful melody rang out from the amplifiers that sat at the stage, his father appeared in a suit and led him to the pastor. Still confused, he walked by his side and in that procession, he saw the entire village lined the sides of the laid out laplap that stretched all the way to the beach.

Just in front of the pastor, they stopped and he turned. His eyes wondered beyond the lined heads, and he could see the door of the sea plane opening. Stepping out to the sandy beach was an angel, covered in white. Beside her was none other than Prudence's father.

At that moment, Telakitahuri knew the wedding that he wanted was now in progress. Mixed feelings of shock, disbelief, excitement, love and nervousness overwhelmed him, bringing him to his knees. He unashamedly wept like a little boy. Everyone around shed a tear for him as his father struggled to get him up on his feet.

In slow motion, the bride made her approach. Finally, he was up on his feet, but the tears of joy continued to well his eyes. Through tears, he watched his angel taking her step one towards him.

He wished she could run up and jump into his arms. But there was her father, who held her hand as if forbidding her.

"Where could my child be?" he thought to himself as his eyes scanned the area.

Walking on the side of the procession was Prudence's mother and as if hiding in the shadow of that woman was Teitione. In her arms, was his bundle of joy.

Not a part of the baby's body could be seen as it was covered in its baby blanket. Then, it became apparent, this was all Teitione, Sione and Prudence's way of surprising him after his father's disagreement to his wedding plans.

Finally, there stood in front of him was Prudence. He lifted her veil, and her tears of joy were flooding her eyes, rolling down her cheeks. Thanks to her oil-based make-up that kept everything intact on a face Telakitahuri always saw there was no need for it.

The pastor stepped in and took over the ceremony.

When the pastor's rituals over their marriage ended with the newlyweds' kiss, Teitione approached with the buddle of joy in her arms.

"He is a boy," she cried, as she handed the baby to his father who was over the moon as he cuddled him for the first time. He removed the blanket that covered the baby and lifting him up for all to see, he chanted.

*"Here lies Teaturiki in my arms.*

*The fruit of my love,*

*And how I cherish his existence.*

*For these veins that run in him*

*Carry my Nukutoa blood.*

*The blood of my forefathers.*

*I lift him high so he can see,*

*Tokorau, Teanake, Tekipu and Telaki.*

*The magnitude of the responsibilities,*

*I brought him to this world to shoulder.*

*Like I never defied my father's call,*

*To be that wall of protection of our islands,*

*From the sea's cruelty.*

*I shout for every Nukutoa child to hear.*

*As its name declared - the island of the giants*

*Stamp your feet into the shifting sand.*

*And declare your unwavering duty,*

*To safeguard and protect your island.*

*Because this blood will not drip into the sea,*

*But lie amongst its forefathers. "*

Telakitahuri's lamentation for the bundle of joy in his arms and his challenge to his son and all other children of Nukutoa brought tears to every islanders' eyes. The memories of their battle against the sea on that fateful day at Nukutapu made some weep openly.

Nukutapu may be gone, but the hearts may take time to heal. There was so many memories that will linger for a long time to come.

As the family retreated to Telakitahuri's house to spend time before their return to Arawa, the villagers celebrated with the spoils that had been provided. No island dishes were available. There laid on the tables were five roasted pigs, a roasted beef, chicken in various dishes and many more dishes that the islanders never had the opportunity to have in abundance.

And, as always present in the islanders' gatherings, was grog, including their beloved kareve.

"Thank you for everything," said Telakitahuri as he hugged Teitione and then Sione.

"I owe you two a lot."

"Don't say a word. This was all Prudence's idea. She even sent Sione to the island to organise everything," revealed Teitione.

"Good men like you, get their blessings even without them knowing," laughed Sione.

Finally, it was time for the sea plane to return to Arawa. That 45 minutes flight should get them there before the place got dark. All the passengers who included those who came with Prudence and her family, Sione and his family and of course Telakitahuri stood on the beach to board the plane.

In numbers, the islanders came forth with hugs, kisses and vaisonis. The overly drunk ones who reeked of kareve were the ones hard to bear.

Eventually, the passengers settled down for their flight, and the plane made its take off.

It circled around the island so that Prudence and her parents could see the extent of the work done. Below they could see the islanders celebrating on the beach. They had a reason to celebrate - like Prudence and Telakitahuri, they truly had resilient hearts. And, the dangers of climate change had been mitigated to some degree.

# The End

# ABOUT THE AUTHOR

Glen Kaiposu Faite is from Mortlock Island in the Autonomous Region of Bougainville. He is a former secondary school teacher with a Degree in Education majoring in Language and Literature. After only eight years of teaching, he abandoned the profession after he felt unjustly treated when he luckily missed his trip back to resume work after his leave.

His department funded return voyage sunk, killing some of the teachers and their children whom, only three weeks prior, they all received their tickets and made their way to home for holiday.

He later worked various jobs while working freelancing as part for his living.

Glen is a passionate writer who likes to write about issues that are closest to his heart. He believes in literature as a tool to inspire change at all levels. In his writing of Resilient Hearts, a story biographically structured, may arouse ideas of resemblance to characters, but it is purely futuristically fictitious with the sole purpose to attract its desired audience.

# ACKNOWLEDGEMENTS

T he journey in making Resilient Hearts an award-winning story would have been more difficult without the people who believed in me and worked hard to make the book a dream come true.

Firstly, I acknowledge the support and encouragement my family gave me during the time of writing; especially my wife Joycelyne Faite. Her contribution with some ideas in settings relating to Bougainville enabled me to successfully complete the story.

I also wish to acknowledge Ed Brumby for his technical edit on the first draft which was half the current story. Your edit gave me confidence to make the story even better.

Whilst I was searching for a publisher, I sought Richard Moyle's advice. In spite of the fact he could not lead me to one, he suggested a few changes that I either adopted or left as they were.

Finally, this publication couldn't have been possible without the vision of the First Nations Writers Festival. Their purpose to promote the writings of Indigenous writers, led to the discovery of this wonderful story of Resilient Hearts. Without this platform, silent voices would not be amplified for the world to hear and literature that sprouted from artistic minds of authors would not be appreciated and loved by an audience.

137

**Editor Contemporary Note:**
https://www.abc.net.au/news/2025-06-01/seawalls-in-the-pacific-climate-change-adaptation/105342110